# Almost Innocent

## Beca Lewis

Perception Publishing

# Contents

# Dedication

*To my mother, Celeste Cecilia Juneau Lewis, who never let me forget she loved me and was proud of the fact that I wrote books she loved to read.*

# Prologue

Marshall Ferguson stood in front of his bedroom mirror and straightened his tie, not judging what he saw. Why would he? Marshall knew that judging himself in any way was never useful or helpful. In fact, from what he had learned during his long tenure as the mayor of Spring Falls, it always led to unpleasantness.

He had seen what judging had done to others, and he had long ago decided not to have that happen to him. This applied to all things. To not judging what he saw in the mirror, to not judging what he had done as mayor to keep the town the beautiful, quiet, and peaceful town that it had become.

Tonight, when he looked in the mirror, he didn't see a sixty-eight-year-old man with a little paunch and a gray beard that hid his jowls. He saw himself as the little boy he had once been. Little had been the word. Too small, too shy, too afraid.

Life had taught him that none of those traits would save him or make him popular. He had worked hard and turned himself into a successful, well-loved, and powerful man. So it was true when he said to the boy in the mirror, "We did it!"

The boy smiled back, gave him a thumbs up, and brushed his hand through his hair before turning away.

As Marshall headed downstairs, careful to keep his hand on the stair rail—his balance was not as good as it used to be—he kept on smiling. He was proud of what he had become. And tonight, he would allow himself to revel in his accomplishments.

Because tonight Spring Falls would honor the man who had brought peace, prosperity, and beauty to the town while keeping the riff-raff out. Tonight he would allow himself to feel the love heaped upon him for what he had done, and who he was. Or who they believed he was.

He would let himself enjoy every minute of the celebration. He would bask in the town's admiration while they still loved him. Because soon that love would be gone. Tomorrow, after a long sleep and a nice breakfast, he was leaving Spring Falls for good. Plenty of money and a new home in a warm, safe place was waiting for him.

At the airport, he would take the book he wrote out of draft mode on Amazon and publish it. It was done, ready to go. The publicity for it was in place. Within a few days, news would trickle out about what he had written. Soon it would become a flood that swept through the town, washing away what people remembered and raising many buried secrets.

After that, very few people—maybe nobody—would call him friend. He didn't care. His book, the one he had been writing for the last forty years, was his best last gift to Spring Falls. A gift where all the secrets he had kept and manipulated to his benefit, and to keep the town a picture of peace and prosperity, would be revealed.

Everyone would read it. He could see it now: the gossip, the worry, the looks of fear and dismay that would spread through the town. Past the town. Into the world.

Everyone would see the dirty underbelly of his life as a mayor. Of course, he called it fiction. But there would be people who would know what he wrote was not fiction. They would see through the story and see the truth. And there would be consequences. Of course, those people would not see his book as a gift. To them, it was a blunt instrument of destruction.

But the gift wasn't for them, it was for the boy in the mirror. And that boy who had been abandoned and bullied was always the only person he had truly cared about. It was a promise he had made to himself, and kept, and now he was ready to tell how he did it.

What Marshall didn't know, and wouldn't have believed even if someone had told him, was that he would never get the chance to publish that book, move to his new home, or witness the reaction to what he wrote. In fact, this would be the last night of his long and illustrious life.

And although Marshall would know who had ended his life for him, for once, all that insider knowledge didn't help him at all.

# One

J udith Zoe and Bruce Dawson stood near the back of the room, little fingers hooked together, and watched the crowd, fully aware that they too were being watched. They were hard to miss.

*Well, Judith is hard to miss,* Bruce thought. Dressed in a long red slinky glittering gown with her hair piled loosely on the top of her head, Judith looked like a goddess.

Bruce knew it wasn't just him who saw Judith that way. The town of Spring Falls both feared and admired Judith. But somehow, he was the one Judith had chosen to stand by her side. He wasn't sure what he had done in life to deserve it, but he was committed to making sure she was always glad she had said 'yes' to him.

As they watched the crowd, standing so close together, him in his new—only worn once before—tuxedo, Bruce thought the two of them looked like the figures that had been on the top of their wedding cake. Although at their wedding, Judith hadn't been wearing a glittering gown, but a soft pink pants suit, her hair encased in a net of lace, her nod to a wedding veil.

The cake had been one of the three concessions they had made for their wedding. The first concession was to how many people attended what was supposed to be a private wedding. Originally, they had planned for just the two of them to stand in front of a Justice of the Peace, and then slip off to a honeymoon. While away, they would send a message to everyone, knowing full well there would be a party for them when they got back.

But Cindy had figured out what they were planning, and that was the end of the secret. The Ruby Sisters had said no, absolutely not, to their two-person wedding. No matter what, they all had to be there.

So instead of just the two of them in front of the Justice of the Peace, they had married with all the Ruby Sisters, plus Booker and Daniel in attendance.

It had been an enormous struggle to keep it that small. Everyone wanted to invite someone else. Cindy wanted Mimi and Janet. Bree wanted Mary and Seth. April wanted to have Robert come back to town to be there. And Marsha wanted to invite Nicky. But somehow they had managed to say "no" to having all those extra people at their wedding.

The hardest one to say "no" to was Nancy, who thought it was her right to be there. After all, she was the one who ran both their offices. But they had to draw the line somewhere, and Nancy was on the other side of the line. She wasn't happy about it either.

Thinking about it now, Bruce thought they might have made a big mistake there. Nancy could make their life miserable if she wanted to. But he was counting on Nancy's innate good nature to forgive them.

Their third concession was letting the mayor marry them. Somehow, Marshall had found out about their appointment at City Hall and insisted on being the one to do the deed. Judith hadn't been surprised that he had found out. Marshall seemed to know everything and everyone in town. It was one of the traits that had made him such a successful mayor.

Now, at his retirement party, Marshall was in rare form. He worked the room, glad-handing everyone, with no special attention paid to anyone. Everyone appeared equal in Marshall's eyes. He had a smile, a nod, knew just the right words to say, and remembered everyone's name. Marshall was a master at working crowds of all sizes.

Marshall's retirement party was not a standard Spring Falls event, where people never really dressed up, even for big events. But somehow Marshall had convinced them all to do something different.

"I want glamor," he had said, and the town had obeyed. Tonight's party was full of sparkles and tuxes. But to Bruce, it was Judith in her sparkling red dress who won the prize for the most glamorous. Although Bruce had to admit to himself that everyone looked lovely. Maybe Marshall was right. The town needed to have this kind of event once in a while.

It was an expensive celebration. But Marshall had paid for all the excesses of the party, saying he didn't want to burden the town. That was pure Marshall. Doing the right thing for everyone, but still getting his way.

So tonight was special, just as Marshall intended. He had insisted that there be no boring speeches and sad faces. He wanted to create a memory no one would ever forget.

So the women glittered, and the men looked elegant in their tuxes. A band played music from the 1970s and people were dancing, laughing, and giggling like the teenagers they once were. A long table overflowing with finger food made sure no one was hungry, and an open bar ensured people stayed happy.

Marshall knew he didn't need to work the crowd the way he always did. He had already won their admiration and respect. And after all, this was his retirement party.

But habits are hard to break, and everyone present was somebody in the town. If he could have had his way, he would have had the whole town at his retirement party. After all, he had served as mayor for the past forty years. This was his town, and he wanted everyone to remember what he had done for it.

Marshall noticed Bruce looking his way and waved. It had given him great pleasure to be the one that married him and Judith. They were now connected to him forever.

Marshall thought that Judith would have made a great mayor. But she had told him emphatically that she had no desire to be a mayor of any town.

Instead, the President of the City Council would take over until they held the election in the fall. Margaret Williams, tall and self-assured, would be more than competent. The town wouldn't fall apart. *Well, maybe it would,* Marshall snickered to himself. *But not because of that.*

Marshall knew it would have been better to wait to retire closer to elections, but he just couldn't bring himself to wait any longer to publish his book. So he had convinced the Council that he was tired and the Council had given in. Actually, Margaret was delighted. She had been waiting for years to become mayor. Now was her chance to shine.

Out of the corner of his eye, Marshall saw Bruce and Judith wave to Booker and Bree, who gestured to a table where Daniel and Cindy were already sitting.

He watched as Judith and Bruce worked their way through the crowd. It took them a while. Everyone wanted to say congratulations. By the time they made it to the table, Marsha and April were at the table.

Marshall smiled to himself. He knew all about the Ruby Sisters. He admired how much they stuck together and thrived despite the difficulties that they had each had. Marshall knew his book would give them all something more to work through together. He hoped they enjoyed it.

After Bruce helped Judith sit, he glanced up and saw Marshall watching them. For a moment, he saw something in Marshall's face he had never seen before, and he felt a chill on the back of his neck. But when he looked again, it was gone. Instead, Marshall beamed at him, gave him a mock salute, waved, and turned away.

"Are you okay?" Judith asked, leaning in.

*Leave it to Judith to notice something different*, Bruce thought.

"Yes, everything is grand," he answered, and for that moment, everything was.

# Two

"Whose house tonight, Judith?" Bruce asked, as he helped Judith into his car, making sure her gown was all the way in and tucked around her legs. Reaching behind the seat he pulled out a blanket and draped it over her lap. It was a frosty night and even with her warm winter coat on, he knew Judith would appreciate the extra warmth.

He often wondered how women managed to remain warm in their elegant gowns, which often left much of their skin exposed. Meanwhile, men were swaddled in layers of clothing. Not that he hadn't enjoyed the beauty of it, sexist or not.

"Let's go to your house," Judith replied.

Bruce smiled and kissed her before shutting the door. Having her in his home filled him with a joy he could hardly express. Within his four walls, Judith allowed herself to be cared for in ways she never did when they were at her place.

To Bruce, caring for Judith was more than just an act of love, it was an honor. She was a woman of undeniable strength and independence, who seldom leaned on others for support.

This new experience of letting someone look after her was an unexplored territory she had decided to venture into with him.

Her choice to trust him with this newfound vulnerability made Bruce feel cherished. He saw it as the greatest gift she could bestow upon him. The fact that this fiercely self-sufficient woman chose to let him in, to take care of her was arguably the most beautiful thing that had ever happened to him.

Before they married, they had discussed if one of them should sell their house and move in with the other. After much honest discussion, they had agreed to keep both houses because both of them loved their homes, although for entirely different reasons.

Judith held a deep, sentimental connection to her house. It was the home she had grown up in, a place teeming with memories from her childhood and the numerous visits from the Ruby Sisters. Over time, she had moulded it into a perfect blend of efficiency and elegance, transforming it according to her personal preferences. The thought of parting with a house overflowing with memories and personal touches was something Judith couldn't bring herself to do..

On the other hand, Bruce's house was new to him. Although smaller than Judith's, with just two bedrooms and a bathroom upstairs, it was ideal for him. The downstairs area had a half bath meant for clients, and an additional room, which he had converted into his office.

This office had direct access to the former living room, now serving as a waiting room. His home might have been newer and less steeped in memories than Judith's, but it fit his needs perfectly, and he had grown to love it.

Bruce appreciated that his home was near the center of town. He could easily walk into town for food or coffee. Plus, his clients liked how easy it was to find him. Bruce also loved living upstairs from his office. It was perfect for getting up in the morning and heading downstairs to meet clients.

So they kept both of their houses, enjoying the choice they could make about where they would spend the night. And even though they were newlyweds, they didn't always spend the night together. Both of them had lived alone for a long time, and enjoyed it. Now they felt as if they had the best of both worlds.

Judith chose Bruce's house tonight because she loved being in his home, where she could let go of managing things. Besides, it felt just like him. Safe and comfortable. No wonder his client base had expanded in the short time he had lived in Spring Falls. Judith knew Bruce was trying to keep his Estate Planning practice small, but she wasn't sure if he would be able to do it.

She knew that in the morning, over the coffee that he would bring to her in bed, they would discuss the evening, so there was no need to tell him what was on her mind now. Their morning talks were one of her favorite times of the day because they talked about everything, from gardens, to work, and what was going on in town.

Sometimes their work overlapped, and if their clients signed a release form, they would often discuss them. Not in a gossipy way, but discussion that would make sure their clients' affairs were neat and tidy. Judith's company took care of their current business and life interests, while Bruce made sure that what they wanted to happen after they passed away was right for everyone involved.

To both of them, their relationship was a business and personal match made in heaven.

Tonight, all Judith wanted to do was to put on some cozy pajamas and climb into bed with Bruce. He had a heated mattress pad which she adored and had gotten one for their bed in her house. On a night like tonight, she needed the warmth. Although the party had been packed with people all wanting to be seen at the party of the year—maybe the decade—the room had been chilly, and she knew she wasn't the only woman cold in her sparse party dress.

However, her desire to retreat to bed and escape her thoughts wasn't merely fueled by the memory of the cold party room. It had more to do with Marshall. There was an unsettling feeling she couldn't quite put her finger on. Certainly, he had behaved in a way that was typical of the Marshall everyone knew, but there was an underlying discrepancy in his demeanor that was difficult to ignore.

Although she could have dismissed her discomfort, attributing it to the unusual circumstances of it being his retirement party, she felt this wasn't the true source of her disquiet. Something about Marshall, something beyond his slightly off manner, had unsettled her, and she couldn't shake off the feeling.

Judith knew Marshall well, and she had always admired his ability to govern the town. It appeared effortless for him. But she knew he practiced appearing to be everyone's best friend. And as he got older, it became easier for Marshall to pull it off because now he looked like everyone's father or even grandfather.

With his prominent belly and thick beard, Marshall could easily blend into any group of men over fifty. Judith often mused over this resemblance. She wondered if men intentionally adopted similar appearances, or if this uniformity was unintentional. Perhaps they weren't even aware of their collective likeness.

Despite priding herself on her keen observational skills, Judith found these resemblances puzzling. Often, she had to give a man a second glance to be sure she had recognized him correctly.

She thought Marshall chose that look on purpose, to both blend in and look warm and friendly. But in all the years she had known him, and that had been a long time, she never fully bought into his "everyone-is-my-friend" act.

She had met Marshall when she was a teenager. She had been trying to figure out what she wanted to do and be in life. Marshall had been mayor for four years, and everyone was already talking about how much he had done for the town, and it inspired her to be like him.

So in her senior year of high school, she applied for and was accepted as an intern in his office. She stayed for three years. The last two years, while she went to the community college, she worked part time as an assistant to his assistant.

From Marshall, she had learned how to pay attention to details while always having the big picture in view. It was Marshall who had taught her how important it was to remain aware of everything that was going on in town.

That skill had kept him in office for forty years. Later, when she applied what she had learned from him to her business, it had thrived. Marshall had also taught her how to deal with conflict. He said there was always a solution that would leave most people, if not happy with the outcome, satisfied enough to agree to move on.

Even though she respected him, Judith had always harbored doubts about Marshall's true intentions. Beneath his facade of being everyone's friend, she suspected there lurked a self-serving motive. But as long as the town prospered, and no harm was done, she had chosen not to dwell on it.

Besides, as of tonight, Marshall was now retired. Were his past motivations really relevant?

As she adjusted the mattress pad's heat to a higher setting and cuddled up to Bruce, Judith pushed away her lingering concerns about Marshall's behavior at his retirement party. *It is probably nothing,* she assured herself. And even if it wasn't, it could certainly wait until morning.

# Three

Pedro Santiago heard a clunk as he pushed the wide broom across the floor. Looking down, he saw something glittering. It was a black and gold cufflink with a symbol on it he didn't recognize.

The other crew members gathered around to look at what he had found, but quickly dismissed it as not important. All they wanted to do was finish cleaning the room so they could have the rest of Sunday to themselves.

Pedro absentmindedly put the cufflink in his pocket while sweeping up the inches of confetti that covered the floor. He thought it must have been quite a celebration. There had been enough balloons to cover the ceiling, and the remnants of the abundance of food were still on the table.

Although the caterer had taken home the unserved food, they had left the dishes behind to be cleaned of food and then stacked. They would pick them up later.

As Pedro cleaned, he couldn't help but resent the wastefulness he was witnessing. He worked two jobs to feed his family, yet here was enough food to sustain them for a week, carelessly left behind by the town's more fortunate residents.

The inequality of it made him mad when he allowed himself to think about it. The company he worked for cared nothing about them. If they made any kind of mistake, or had to take a day off for family or health reasons, they were at risk of being fired.

And the town's disregard for its less fortunate members extended beyond waste. Many of his friends and families, including his own, were now being forced out of their homes to make way for a new, upscale housing development. No one seemed to care where the current residents would go.

He eyed the left-over food, considering packing some into his lunch box to take home to his family. However, the risk of getting caught and losing his job was too high a price to pay.

He continued his work, the mystery cufflink in his pocket forgotten for now, his mind too occupied with worrying about where he would be living in just a few months.

· • • • • • • • • • ·

"That was an amazing party, wasn't it?" Bree asked Booker.

"It was. And uneventful," he answered, stretching his long legs out under the kitchen table, waiting for the breakfast that Bree was making. When they were at her house, she cooked; at his house he cooked or he ordered in. He had to admit they ordered in more than he cooked, but Bree said she didn't mind.

"Uneventful?" Bree laughed. "With all those people there pretending to be the best of friends, all the food, all the alcohol? Plus, all the gossip floating around the room. It was uneventful?"

Bree was teasing. She knew what Booker had meant. There had been no trouble that he, as sheriff of Spring Falls, would have had to step in to handle. Although Booker had been officially off duty, she knew that to him off duty only meant he wasn't getting paid. Booker was always on alert. Even last night when he was supposed to let himself relax a little and enjoy himself.

And they had. They had eaten far too much and drank multiple glasses of flavored sparkling water. Booker never drank alcohol because he believed that his job meant he could be called out at any moment. And Bree never drank because of the memories of her mother's drinking.

Bree and Booker had chatted with almost everyone. And like everyone else there, they had thanked the mayor for his service. Forty years was a long time, and during that time, the town had prospered. Something Marshall let no one forget. He was always subtle about it. Even so, he made sure people remembered it was him who had renewed Spring Falls.

And, like Booker who was always on guard and paying attention, Bree was also always paying attention. But not for the same reason. She was watching for ideas, for stories.

Bree observed how people behaved and what they said. She listened for stories that could end up being in a book she was writing or inspire another plot line. Bree always disguised the stories enough that no one recognized them officially, but it helped her books feel more real to people.

Last night's party had supplied her with a few ideas, which she had jotted down on the slips of paper she always kept with her. She had learned that she needed to write ideas down as soon as they came to her, because otherwise she'd forget all about them. Instead, she would be left with a nagging feeling that there was something she should be remembering.

At the party, she had to stuff the papers into the tiny sparkling bag she was carrying. Her regular purse would not have fit in with the gown she was wearing. She couldn't remember the last time she had been so dressed up and wondered if she would ever be again. *But at least I'll have a dress to wear, if I do,* Bree thought.

Now she was in sweatpants and a long sweatshirt that said "Writer" on it. It was a gift from the Ruby Sisters after her last book was published. They always celebrated with her. Knowing how quickly life could change, they made it a practice to celebrate even the smallest of victories.

Given that it was Sunday and Booker was off duty, she was taking a day off from writing. They planned on spending the entire day together. Maybe doing nothing. So far, it was going that way. Outside it was spitting snow, but it wasn't enough for either of them to have to get up and shovel.

Addie, Booker's dog, was curled up under the table, lying on Booker's feet. Addie was getting old and sometimes Bree worried how Booker would handle Addie not being around anymore. She hoped that wouldn't be for a few more years, anyway.

But today, they were warm and happy together, and Bree didn't feel like bringing up her nagging feeling that something was going on with Marshall. She knew he was leaving for a vacation today as a gift to himself, and she hoped the snow wouldn't keep the planes on the ground.

Marshall definitely deserved a vacation. As far as Bree knew, he hadn't taken more than a day off in all the years he was the town's mayor.

However, Bree felt strangely uneasy when she thought about Marshall. Something had been different last night. But she decided that it wasn't worth worrying about. Today was a day of rest and she was going to take it.

# Four

Booker and Bree were not the only ones who had chosen to make Sunday a day of rest. Every Ruby sister was doing just that in her own way.

At the Ruby House, Marsha Martin was doing what she most loved to do every Sunday morning. Make plans. Because although Sunday mornings were a day of rest from teaching, they weren't a day of rest for Marsha's mind.

She loved the open day, with nothing to do so she could plan. So while April slept in, she sat at the kitchen table with her tablet and made lists.

She didn't love lists for lists' sake the way Bree and Judith seemed to, especially Bree, whose lists of things to do took her breath away. Marsha had no idea how Bree managed to get everything done on her list. If she had a list like that, it would make her crazy.

Marsha's lists were more circular. Having recently discovered a mind mapping app and the joy of using the colors available on her tablet, Marsha's lists now swirled around the page, much like a dance.

She couldn't wait for April to wake up so she could talk about her plans for the Ruby House. Dance and drama lessons were going well, along with her daily yoga classes. But sooner or later, she was going to need to hire someone to help her.

But that would be a decision that she and April would need to make together. Plus, Marsha knew that April was going to need more space if she wanted to expand her design business. Perhaps they could put a building up in the backyard?

Marsha was full of ideas and was ready to do something about them. She needed April to wake up so they could talk about it.

But April Zane wasn't sleeping. Lying in bed, she was reliving the trip she had taken with her son, Robert. Having seen so many beautiful places, the trip had re-inspired her desire to make beautiful spaces for people, and now she had a new client.

Last night at Marshall's retirement party, Marshall had asked her if she would redesign his house now that he would spend more time at it. He had asked her to come by after he returned from vacation.

April had been in his house before and already had ideas about what she could do. She had asked him if he knew what he wanted, and he had said no. He would follow her direction. Redoing the Mayor's home was a dream come true. She couldn't wait to get started.

Cindy was trying to figure out how to talk to Daniel about him moving in with her.

Despite their relationship being only a few months old, she felt that the time had come for a deeper commitment. After all, they had endured numerous tests, including the revelation that she was the artist behind the paintings that had brought fame to Daniel's father, Cedric Jacobs.

They survived the storm of Steven's arrest for giving deadly drugs that led to Daniel's father's death and Steven's failure to ask for help when Cedric collapsed. Now Cindy felt a sense of inevitability about taking the next step—moving in together. It was only a matter of deciding when it would happen.

Cindy thought that the time was now, although the change for her would be profound. She had been accustomed to solitude her entire life, while cherishing the dream of sharing a relationship like the one she now had with Daniel. However, she had surrendered that dream at one point, resigning herself to a life of independent loneliness.

Yet, life had a surprise in store for her, transforming her dream into a reality. Now she craved a deeper connection, longing to start each day with Daniel by her side, making their relationship part of her everyday life. She knew that Daniel shared her desire for this new level of companionship.

However, she knew that Daniel, like her, had always lived a solitary life. She knew that transitioning from their respective lives of solitude to a shared life would require adjustments and patience. The prospect of being together all day, every day, was something she wanted, and yet she wasn't sure if they could adjust to that new way of life.

Cindy had thought about suggesting that they do what Booker and Bree and Bruce and Judith were doing, and keep separate homes. But she knew that's not what she wanted. So today was the day she was going to suggest that he give up his apartment and move in. They'd figure out a way for Daniel to have his own space. Besides, she was at the studio almost every day, so he'd have the house to himself.

But she was worried that he might not like the quiet of Spring Falls after living in New York City his whole life.

What Cindy didn't know was that Daniel had already thought through what it would be like living with Cindy. He wanted to, but he knew himself well enough to know he needed his own space. And although he loved Spring Falls, Cindy was right. He also loved the excitement of New York.

He thought he had a solution to the problem. Today was the day he was going to bring it up and see what Cindy thought. He was fairly sure that she would like his suggestion. Still, it was a risk, and he was stalling.

So now they were in the living room, sitting side by side on the plushy maroon couch that faced the front window watching the snow fall, both of them wondering how to talk about what was on their minds. In the end, it was Cindy who brought up the subject, not able to contain it any longer.

Daniel's solution was so perfect that Cindy got up and danced around the living room, her blond hair, now laced with strands of gray that she was letting alone—proud now of who she had become—flying behind her.

As he watched Cindy spin around the living room, Daniel remembered the first time he had seen her. She was twenty, and he had been ten. She was his father's student, caught up in his web of lies.

Now they were both free. His father was dead. Her teacher's lies had been revealed. And Cindy had become what she had always dreamed of being. She was a recognized artist. Daniel smiled, happy that Cindy had liked his solution. Not just liked it, loved it.

He would represent her in the art world, which meant he would need to spend some time in New York. Steven, who was out of jail for what had happened between him and his father, could show him the ropes. That way, he could still have New York, but his home would be here in Spring Falls with Cindy.

Cindy danced over to him, pulled him to his feet and together they flew around the living room, finally collapsing onto the couch together, laughing with happiness, thinking that they deserved it and from now on life would only get better.

For a fleeting moment, Cindy thought about Marshall and wondered where he had hung the painting she had recently painted for him. She had added one tiny touch to it, one that only he would notice because he had asked her to put it there. It was a symbol he had shown her on a piece of paper. She didn't know what it meant, but he said it was important to him, so she had agreed.

Last night at his retirement party, Marshall had once again expressed his gratitude to Cindy for the painting and extended an invitation to her to visit and see where he had hung it once he returned from his vacation. Cindy wondered whether that would be when Marshall would unravel the meaning behind the mysterious symbol.

But of course, Cindy, like everyone else, was unaware that Marshall never intended to return from his vacation.

Now settling back into the couch, coffee cups in hand, watching the snow fall, Daniel by her side, Cindy hoped Marshall had made it out of town before the snow, and was already heading towards his vacation in a warm sunny place.

She didn't know that not only was Marshall not in a warm sunny place. Instead, he was very, very cold.

# Five

On Monday morning, Judith carried on with her usual routine, starting with meeting Cindy at the coffee shop where she found her beaming with happiness. As soon as they had their coffee, Cindy poured out her exciting news. Daniel would move in with her but would also keep his apartment in New York so he could handle the sale of her paintings.

"It's the perfect solution," Cindy said, and Judith nodded and smiled in agreement, thinking Cindy's news was the perfect start of the week. Then they moved on to discussing Marshall's party.

"It was like everyone who runs the town was there," Cindy said, and again Judith nodded in agreement. She didn't mention that she had thought Marshall had been acting strangely, not wanting to mar Cindy's happiness. Besides, she didn't even know what she meant by acting strangely.

A few minutes later, Daniel arrived, looking as happy as Cindy. Judith motioned for him to come sit with them, congratulated and hugged them both, and then left them there to work out the logistics of their decision.

Leaving the coffee shop, Judith pulled her winter coat close around her. She kept her head bowed down against the blast of winter wind that whipped through the streets along with a smattering of wet snow while smiling into the scarf wrapped around the lower half of her face. All the Ruby Sisters were happy. Life was good, although, at the moment, very cold.

At the office, she hung her coat on the hook by the front door, letting it drip onto the rubber mat below it, shucked off her winter boots, and slipped into her office shoes.

Nancy handed her a cup of coffee and the agenda for the Monday morning call on Zoom with all the independent attorneys and contractors that worked with her. Not for the first time, Judith wondered how she could ever manage without Nancy.

She didn't think she'd ever have to find that out. Although Nancy and Steven—despite his actions towards Daniel's father—had kept up a relationship, Nancy had assured Judith that she had no intention of leaving Spring Falls or her job. It wasn't until Nancy had assured her she was staying that Judith realized she had been worried.

Smiling again at Nancy, Judith glanced at the agenda and headed into her office, pushing the office door open with her hip, the coffee and agenda occupying her hands. She was looking forward to the call, but then she always looked forward to these calls. *What's not to like,* she thought. Putting things in order and making things right was fun for her, and it was a joy to be part of a team that did all of that for Spring Falls.

Besides, she enjoyed each member of her team as a person, and loved the community feeling they had built together. However, today she was a little nervous because there would be a new member of her team on the call. How Tanner Foster would fit in would determine whether she would ask him to return.

Tanner was a young accountant who had already built a small private practice. But he had contacted Judith, expressing a desire to be part of something bigger than just himself.

He and Judith had met a few times before she agreed to let him come to a Monday morning call. She had stipulated that he could take part in the meetings, work with her privately, but she wouldn't assign anyone new to him until she got used to working with him, and the group had accepted him.

Tanner had agreed, explaining that he often had questions about things that came up with clients and thought that working with Judith and her community of accountants and bookkeepers would be of great help to him.

He assured Judith that he understood that he was on probation. Even though every member of Judith's team had their own practice, they were committed to the standards that Judith set. They shared information about clients, if their interests overlapped, so it was critical that everyone was honest and upright. So if the team didn't trust Tanner, then he would not be invited to return.

When Tanner had called requesting a meeting, Judith had looked into who he represented and discovered one of his clients was a developer in town. For that reason alone, she was happy to have Tanner join her team. Spring Falls was her town, and she wanted it to remain the beautiful place that it was.

Judith knew a developer motivated only by profit often built ugly things and hurt people in the process, and she didn't want that in Spring Falls. If she could stop them behind the scenes, with the help of her team, she would do it. Each member of her team believed in fair practices and sustainability for every person living in Spring Falls.

Judith knew that keeping Spring Falls beautiful and providing a good life for every citizen was a tall order. But it was something she thought she could do, and anyone who knew her believed she could do it too.

Closing the door behind her, Judith paused for a moment to take in her office. She loved this space. It was always orderly and clean, and as beautiful as she could make it with a vase of flowers, one of Cindy's paintings, and soft lighting. Of course, there was also a ring light on her computer, so she was lit well for the call, but that was a necessity in today's world.

Closing the blinds behind her so only a soft glow formed behind her head, she turned on the computer and set up the meeting.

Tanner was there the minute she logged on.

"I'm so glad I got you before everyone else comes on," he said. Judith thought he looked a little pale.

"Are you alright?"

"Yes. At least I think so. Could we talk after this? I could come by your office later."

Judith glanced at her appointment schedule that Nancy had left by her computer and found a time later that day.

By then, other people started filtering in and Tanner did what she requested, listened, asked a few questions, and shared a little about who he was. She could see that he made a good impression on the group.

Ninety minutes later, they had covered everyone's questions and concerns, and Judith was ready for a break. Although she had loved every minute, she found the meetings exhausting. Nancy always scheduled breathing room after every Monday morning meeting so that Judith would have time to herself.

Lying back on her couch, Judith closed her eyes and let herself briefly float away. It was an important part of her day. Often, she would wake up with solutions to things that were bothering her. Today she hoped she'd have a better sense of what was different about Marshall on Saturday night.

She hoped he was enjoying himself on his warm vacation because Tanner had asked a question in the meeting that worried her, and she thought Marshall might be connected with it. She couldn't wait to question Tanner and Marshall about it.

# Six

Emma Drake spent a few minutes warming up before starting her run. Her mother thought Emma was crazy to go out running in this kind of weather. But Emma felt she knew herself well enough to know when she needed to get out of the house for a run. Otherwise, moods built up, and that was never a good thing.

Besides, the wind and snow had stopped, and now it was just cold. A few minutes of running would warm her up. Besides, she wasn't careless about running in this kind of weather. She had chains on her running shoes and was wearing the warm weather gear her uncle Daniel had given her for her birthday. Or maybe it was for Christmas. It was probably a combination of both, since she knew how expensive each item was.

Emma had always hated having her birthday so close to Christmas, but with her newly-developed sixteen-year-old wisdom, she decided she would be grateful she got to celebrate twice in such a beautiful season.

But now it was February, and it was not her favorite month. It was the mud and slush mixed with icy winds and snow season. She couldn't wait until March arrived. At least in March, despite some snow, and the mud and slush, there were hints of spring.

On one of their walks in the woods together, Bree had told Emma that there were hints of spring in February too. You just had to look. Birds were searching out nesting sites, and tiny shoots of early spring bulbs were visible.

But today Emma wasn't looking for signs of spring; she was looking for inspiration for her art. A few months into Cindy's art classes, Emma had started looking at the world entirely differently. Now she saw a world filled with beauty in small and unexpected places. Now she could look at tree lines and building lines against the sky and could find beauty in both.

What she wanted to learn was how to express in her art the feelings that all that beauty in unexpected places brought out in her.

Cindy had told Emma to try out many styles, to not get locked into anything. That's why they not only painted in art class, but they sculpted, drew with charcoal, made collages, and did weavings. Emma thought Cindy was scouring the internet for ways to make art and then making them try it out.

At first, Emma didn't like it. She wanted to paint with actual paint, not watercolors. She hadn't wanted to sculpt or stick stuff onto cardboard. But she had noticed that trying all those mediums had changed how she expressed herself. Not just in her paintings, but in her dance classes with Marsha.

Even Marsha had noticed the difference in her. The other day, Marsha complimented Emma on how well she was doing in ballet class. Emma thought some of that improvement could also be attributed to the yoga class she and her mother took together once a week from Marsha.

Life was so much better than it had been when they first arrived in Spring Falls. She had made a few friends her age, something she had never had before, and the Ruby Sisters kept providing opportunities for her. Plus, she had an uncle now, someone she had admired even before she found out they were related.

Daniel was like having a fairy godfather. He had bought them a house in town and had transferred some of the money from his father's estate to them.

She still worked part time at Cindy's gallery, even though they could pay for her classes now, but she liked the work. Mimi and Janet were showing her how Cindy's art business ran, and she thought it was fascinating. Everything in her life was better than she ever thought possible.

As Emma stepped outside, she yelled back to her mother that she was going, and heard her mother yell back, "Stay safe!"

At her mother's request, Emma had put the Find A Friend app on her phone so her mom would know where she was when she was out exploring. It seemed a minor concession in return for being on her own much more, and secretly she was glad that someone always knew where she was. It did feel safer that way.

Today Emma was heading off to what Judith called the Nature Safety Zone, because it was a place where all nature could flourish. It was a band of land that would eventually circle the town, keeping Spring Falls a beautiful place to live. It was really called the Green Zone, but Emma liked Judith's name better.

When Emma first found out about it, she thought it was a joke. What town would keep part of its valuable land safe from developers? She and her mother had lived in many ugly places. Towns and cities where developers had built ugly buildings, strip malls, rows of look-alike blocky houses. Sometimes it hurt her just to look at the things around her as they drove down the street.

It was one reason she had fallen in love with Spring Falls. It tried and succeeded, for the most part, to be beautiful. Sure, there were places that needed to be fixed up, but on the whole, the town was beautiful. There were entire neighborhoods that felt like wonderful places to live. Each house was unique and yet fit in with one another. *Like the people I've met,* Emma thought.

Judith had explained that the circle wasn't complete yet, though. Some of the land was still owned by families. What Judith and other members of the Green Zone Trust community had done was convince each of those families to deed the land at their deaths to the Trust that protected the land. If they wanted to, they could also sell the land to the Trust while they were alive but continue to live on it for the rest of their lives.

It took a lot of money to do this, all of which came from donations, because no one would get wealthy from the land. Plus, it needed to be maintained, which was also expensive. Emma knew Judith was instrumental in getting the donations for the purchases and the maintenance, and she was the treasurer of the committee that watched over the Trust. Judith was constantly promoting the value of keeping Spring Falls beautiful to her many clients.

Emma had decided to make it her business to know that strip of land well. And when she got famous, she would dedicate a portion of her sales from her art to the Trust. It was something she knew Cindy had set up in her business, and Emma assumed that every Ruby Sister was doing the same thing.

As for being famous, Emma had no doubt she would be. She was only sixteen, but she had known who she was and what she wanted since she was a little girl, and now she no longer needed to hide it from anyone.

Emma knew her mom would say she was still a little girl, but she knew she wasn't. She was young, yes, but not a little girl. Bree told her she had the heart of a lion. Emma wasn't exactly sure what that meant, but she liked it. She would repay all the kindness the town had shown her since they had moved in by making sure it remained beautiful.

With one last glance back at the house they were living in now, a house that Daniel had bought and Cindy and Seth were renovating for them, she waved to her mother standing in the window, and headed towards the Green Zone. She wanted to know the Green Zone well, and she would do it one section at a time.

# Seven

I t was the cleaning crew hired by the realtor who found
him. According to the schedule, they had arrived at 10:00
a.m. Monday morning to prepare the house for sale—dusting,
scrubbing, and ensuring the property was in tip-top condition.

The realtor was the only person in on the secret that Marshall
would never return to Spring Falls. That while the town prepared
for his retirement party, he prepared to leave them forever.

What the realtor was blissfully unaware of was the sly
satisfaction that Marshall harbored about his secret. He had been
relishing the fact that he was departing town, leaving behind what
would become a chaotic storm. This storm, this mess, would
unravel the moment the first reader flipped open his book. And
when it did, it would take far more than a diligent cleaning crew
to restore peace and order.

For months, Marshall had slowly sold everything of value in his
home. He never had visitors in his house. It was a rule of his. He
held all his meetings in public spaces. His home was his sanctuary.
No business was allowed in it. This rule had ensured that on the

off chance someone dropped by, they would not have noticed the changes as he and his realtor staged it for the sale.

By the time Marshall had gone to his retirement party, there was nothing in the closets or cupboards. Nothing personal remained in the house but the clothes in his suitcase, and his computer. That was all he needed for his new life. Where he was going, he would be a wealthy man and he would buy what he needed when he got there.

For Marshall, the most tantalizing aspect of his impending journey was the promise of a warmer climate. There would be no need for a cumbersome overcoat or the insulation of snow boots. No more laborious snow shoveling or the endless mowing of lawns. He would be truly free. He would hire help for any necessary tasks.

Marshall was looking forward to shedding the facade of a modest lifestyle sustained on a meager mayor's salary. Now, he could finally indulge in a life of comfort and ease. At first, he had planned to live an unassuming life when he moved, but soon realized that he wanted to be known as a very wealthy, self-made man. No one had ever given him anything. He earned every penny, and he deserved it.

Marshall had a plan. He'd wear his heavy winter coat to the airport, a symbol of his past life, and then simply discard it in the waiting room. The act would be akin to shedding his skin, much like a snake. This analogy pleased Marshall, for he knew he was indeed a snake. Not an ordinary garden variety, but a poisonous and dangerous one.

That he had slithered unnoticed through the community of Spring Falls, subtly poisoning their town, was a source of astonishment even to him. He had successfully executed his venomous plot without a hint of suspicion. He had gotten away with it. No one knew what he had been doing for forty years.

That wasn't quite true. A few individuals had been privy to the darker aspects of Marshall's activities, but only because they assisted him. Or because he bribed them to help by holding their crimes against them. They remained silent because their complicity served their interests. Some of them, Marshall felt, were as serpentine as he was.

He pictured their meetings together as a gathering of snakes, coiling around each other, hissing, flicking out forked tongues, and rattling their tails. Yet they never dared to bite him. He was the dominant serpent in this reptilian hierarchy, and they were well aware of it.

He had pledged to guard their secrets, and they had every reason to reciprocate. It was a code of honor among thieves. But they lacked the foresight to realize that once he had ensured his own safety from any fallout, he would expose them, reveling in their naivete.

That was his plan. And it was a good one. There was no reason for Marshall to suspect that his plan would backfire, that his forty years of service and the admiration he had inspired would all dissolve in an instant.

So when the cleaning crew found him at the bottom of his stairs—his winter coat spread out underneath him, the red silk lining hiding the pool of blood that surrounded him, his eyes wide open—they screamed, and then cried. And continued crying as they called 911. Their beloved mayor was dead.

Later, describing the scene to Bree, Booker told her that Marshall looked astonished. And he was. In that last minute, as life drained out of him, Marshall realized he had misjudged the person who had pushed him down the stairs. And all the work he had put into becoming a wealthy man was for naught. He couldn't take it with him.

In the final moments of his life, Marshall could only watch as his attacker absconded with his computer and his carefully constructed novel, and he knew he had failed. Those he had intended to expose would continue to thrive in their positions. The possibility even loomed that one of them might step into his shoes and continue what he had begun.

The individual who now possessed his computer held all the necessary information to devastate countless lives. The illicit wealth they could amass from Marshall's painstaking efforts felt like the ultimate betrayal. His life's work would become someone else's tool for personal gain.

*Not fair*, was Marshall's last thought on earth.

# Eight

The news rippled through the town like a shock wave. Within an hour, the death of their beloved mayor had become the source of discussion everywhere. Word had gotten out initially through a member of the cleaning crew who, overwhelmed by the shocking discovery, had confided in a friend. From there, the news spread like wildfire. Neighbors huddled on porches, texts spread with lightning speed, and the town's gossip mill went into overdrive.

However, the only information available was that the mayor had been found dead, presumed to have fallen down the stairs. By the time Booker reached the scene, it seemed that half of Spring Falls was already aware of the devastating news. Any attempt to control the media narrative was futile at this point. The news was too far spread, the town too abuzz.

What Booker hoped for now was that, amidst this frenzy, they could glean some valuable information about Marshall's family. As the media turned its spotlight on the mayor's sudden death, it seemed inevitable that it would uncover more about his private life.

As the media delved into Marshall's background in search of a story, Booker hoped they would discover relatives of Marshall's. Because Marshall had always been private about his past life, no one knew anything about his family. As far as Booker knew, Marshall had never married and had no children.

Although Booker had never become a close friend of Marshall's, they were friendly to each other. After all, they often did business together, working to keep the town safe.

However, one night, Booker had found Marshall in one of the town's bars. He had stopped in to hear a local band and found Marshall sitting at a table in the back of the room. They had shared a few drinks, and as they sat together, Marshall had shared a little about his life. His parents had died when he was eighteen and he was the only child.

When the band took a break and they could hear each other better, Booker had asked Marshall where he grew up.

"Here. In Spring Falls, like you," he replied. "The town was different back then."

Booker thought back to his youth in Spring Falls. Fifteen years younger than Marshall, he only remembered the town as a great place to grow up.

"How so?"

"Hard to explain," Marshall answered. "Dirtier maybe. Not as charming as it is now. Not as nice a place to grow up as it has become."

"Well, a lot of that has to do with you, Marshall," Booker had said. "You've been mayor for a long time. If things have changed for the better, much of that has to do with you."

Marshall smiled and nodded, and they'd clinked glasses. That had been years before, and Spring Falls had only gotten better since then. Booker thought that the town had lost a great man, and people would mourn him for a long time.

After the coroner arrived, and the body was removed, Booker and his team walked through the house. At first, Booker had thought the death was simply an accident. Marshall, in his hurry to get to his vacation, had tumbled down the stairs. They had found his suitcase close to his body. He must have tripped, and then the weight of the suitcase kept the momentum going.

But soon it became apparent that something was wrong. Searching the house, they realized it was empty. Booker's first thought was that the house looked staged. And when the realtor showed up, ready to install the lock on the door and put the For Sale sign in the yard, his suspicions were confirmed.

It was only then that a chilling thought gnawed at Booker. It was possible that Marshall's death was not accidental. There were anomalies that he couldn't ignore. A seemingly innocuous yet glaring clue nudged him toward this conclusion. The notable absence of Marshall's computer. The device, which seemed as much a part of Marshall as his own arm, was nowhere to be found.

This realization cast a new, unsettling light on the situation. Someone else had been in the house. Marshall was skipping town. Why? Did someone push him down the stairs? Why?

None of it made any sense. Why would someone kill a man as beloved by the town as Marshall was? The puzzle pieces didn't seem to fit together. None of it fit what Booker knew about Marshall.

Unconsciously brushing his hair back, something everyone knew he did when he was confused or worried, Booker studied the stairs with the pool of blood at the bottom that had come from the wound on the back of Marshall's head—apparently caused by Marshall hitting his head on the edge of a step as he fell. And just in case Marshall was still hanging around listening, Booker promised him he'd find out what had happened and why.

The next phase of the investigation was just beginning, and the answers to what happened to Marshall would unravel secrets that

Booker could not have foreseen or believed. Marshall was a hero in Spring Falls, and nothing Booker knew about Marshall had ever made him think otherwise.

But then, as the truth was revealed, everyone would shake their heads and say it wasn't possible. But it was. Marshall had fooled them all until he couldn't any longer.

# Nine

Judith was still lying on the couch when Nancy poked her head into the room. Normally, she would have closed the door and slipped away, but this time she knew what she had to tell Judith couldn't wait.

Hesitating in the doorway, she tried to think of the best way to wake Judith up, but was saved from doing so when Judith, with her eyes still closed, asked, "What's up?"

"Sorry to wake you up, but there is something you need to know."

"Not sleeping. Thinking, and resting my eyes."

Hearing the tone of Nancy's voice, Judith sat up and, patting the seat beside her, said, "What's wrong? Sit. Can I get you something?"

Sitting beside Judith, her head bent down, trying to hide her tears, Nancy whispered, "Marshall is dead."

"What do you mean, he's dead? He's on vacation."

As Nancy repeated what she knew—that Marshall had been found dead at the bottom of his stairs—Judith kept shaking her head. It couldn't be true. He was headed for a well-deserved vacation. He had promised that when he returned, he'd help her with a project she was planning, converting one of the empty office buildings in town into a homeless shelter.

Although they didn't have a homeless problem, Judith suspected that there were people who hid the fact that they were on the streets or living in cars. She was determined to help anyone who might struggle with being unhomed. She thought that word was stupid. If you didn't have a home, then you were homeless. But no matter what it was called, Judith felt it was wrong. Judith had planned to work with Marshall to gather funds for the renovation of the building and turn it into small apartments. But it would also have a common room for training and computers that everyone could use.

And she knew there were other programs that Marshall had promised to help with when he returned. One of them was a program Cindy had started. She was teaching anyone who was interested how to make something she could sell online for them. Cindy was thinking about quilts or weaving, but one woman had asked about making chef's aprons. She had made them for all the chefs at ParaTi's and when she found out how much they loved wearing them, she thought she could turn it into a business with Cindy's, Mimi's, and Janet's help.

In fact, Judith thought that what Marshall had lined up to do when he returned from vacation was going to keep him busier than being a mayor.

All those thoughts flew by in Judith's head. As she stood, she felt groundless and unsteady. Without Marshall helping the town as he always had, what would happen?

It was so inconceivable, she asked again, "Are you sure?"

Nancy nodded. "Yes, my friend at the paper called me. The news is spreading like wildfire. What do you want to do?"

Judith held up a finger for Nancy to wait a minute, picked up her phone and called Booker. When he didn't answer, she tapped her foot for a minute and then sent a text to all the Ruby Sisters, including Booker, Bruce, and Daniel.

"Did you hear? What do you know?"

A flurry of "yes, no, what do you mean, I don't know anything" flooded in. Another flurry revealed who didn't know what had happened. But no one knew more than that. Booker didn't answer.

In fact, seeing the flood of texts, Booker had frowned, and then turned off the sound on his phone. He couldn't have this. Not now.

Sighing, he finally texted back, "I can't answer any of this, and you'll have to leave me out of these conversations for now." Adding a second later: "Please."

Seeing Booker's answer, Judith knew it was more than what Nancy said. Marshall didn't just fall down the stairs. Something else happened, and she would find out what it was. Marshall wasn't a close friend, but she had known him well enough. Not only was he her first boss, he had changed Spring Falls for the better, for which she, and she knew all the townspeople, would be forever grateful.

Picking up her purse and fluffing her hair out from where it had flattened when she lay down, Judith said, "Cancel my appointments, please. Probably all that would happen anyway would be gossip about Marshall. I'm heading out."

Nancy didn't need to ask Judith where she was going. She had worked with Judith long enough to know that she wouldn't be able to leave this alone. She'd have to know more, and she would gnaw at the puzzle of why Marshall was dead until she found out the answers.

At the door, with her coat and boots on, Judith turned and looked at her office. It looked the same as it always did. And she wondered how that could be true. A hero of Spring Falls was dead.

Something should have happened. A thunderclap, an earthquake. Something.

Not trusting herself to speak, Judith waved her fingers at Nancy, who was now standing at her desk, her phone tucked between her shoulder and ear, doing what she always did. Taking care of things.

Nancy nodded back. What was there to say? Nothing could be exactly the same after this. Marshall held the town together. Who was going to do that now that he was gone?

# Ten

Tanner heard the news while seated in one of his favorite diners in Spring Falls. The diner was tucked behind the main buildings downtown, on the corner of two well-maintained alleys. The eatery was a popular haunt among the local college students, and its bustling energy was further brought to life by its spirited owner, Margaret Williams, someone he worked with on the Town Council.

He'd always sit in the back—thinking—trying to be as invisible as possible. Or at least hoping he was less noticeable sitting in the back. He didn't look much older than the crowd that was usually there, but he still felt a little self-conscious, as if he didn't belong. Feeling that he was an impostor wasn't unusual, nor was feeling as if he didn't belong. Both were as familiar to him as the color of his eyes when he looked in the mirror. He had long ago stopped wondering if everyone felt that way. It was hard enough to deal with it himself.

For as long as Tanner could remember, he had struggled to look as if he was sure of himself. He had learned the hard way that pretending he was confident was a necessary survival skill. But for him, it was almost always an act. One he had perfected over the years, but still within himself, he was always sure that who he was could never be enough. For anything.

So, on the Zoom call with Judith and her team that morning, he had said as little as possible in case he screwed up somehow. Instead, he nodded and smiled and made notes on his iPad, which he used instead of paper. Like Marshall's computer, it was always wherever he was.

He was good at keeping notes. Actually, when he was being kind to himself, he admitted he was good at quite a few things. He was an excellent student. He studied hard. He was a good accountant, going over everything until he was sure it was right. He was even a good ballroom dancer, having once dated a woman who insisted they take ballroom lessons together. She hadn't stayed around, but the love of ballroom dance had.

As he savored the best Mexican food he had ever eaten (not that he had much experience with any other Mexican food, having lived a fairly secluded life), he reviewed the call with Judith. It amazed him how well she managed the meeting. Each person had a chance to talk and ask a question. Then someone else would share what they knew or thought about the situation.

The discussions were fascinating, and he learned more in those ninety minutes about working with clients than he thought possible. Although he had questions, they weren't ones he could voice out loud until he knew he could trust everyone.

In fact, he thought he might never talk to anyone other than Judith about what was bothering him. Tanner knew that he'd have to do it soon, but as usual, he was stalling. What if getting help from Judith was the wrong thing?

Having taken his last bite of food, savoring the flavors as long as he could, Tanner was closing up his iPad, ready to go to his office, when Margaret rushed over to him as if the restaurant was on fire.

Tanner had met Margaret not long after he moved to Spring Falls. For some reason, she noticed him. Later, she told him it was because he seemed familiar. But after trying to figure out if they had ever met before, they gave up and decided it was just one of those things.

And it was because of Margaret and all the people she knew that he had ended up on Spring Fall's Town Council. She had picked him, she said, because they needed someone young, and new to Spring Falls so he would see it with fresh eyes. At first he had said no, but she kept insisting, pushing almost every button he had about doing the right thing.

Campaigning was one of the worst things he'd ever put himself through, but Tanner had done what Margaret asked of him to get elected. He shook hands, smiled at press gatherings and somehow had ended up on the Town Council, the youngest member they ever had, as they constantly reminded him.

Once he was elected, Margaret had made it clear that she didn't want Tanner to be part of Judith Zoe's stable of accountants. At the time, he had agreed. That was over a year ago. He had never asked Margaret why. Perhaps she thought it would be a conflict of interest.

But as his client base grew including some small businesses in town, he realized he was over his head. He had heard about Judith Zoe as soon as he moved to Spring Falls. Imposing, slightly intimidating, but everyone always said that Judith knew right from wrong and fought for it.

Tanner wasn't sure he saw things that clearly. He needed guidance. And that's why he approached Judith, hoping she'd say yes, knowing Margaret would not be happy with him. Which meant he was more than a little worried about telling her he was now part of Judith's team. It would be hard to explain to Margaret that he needed more expertise with one of the clients he had, and that's why he asked to join Judith's community of accountants and bookkeepers.

Truthfully, Tanner thought he would be a better Town Council member if he knew more people and more about how the town functioned. He wasn't particularly impressed with the rarefied view he believed the Council had of Spring Falls. Yes, he was getting to know Spring Falls, but Tanner felt that there was much more going on that he needed to know to be good at his job as a Council member.

He might be insecure about who he was, but Tanner knew himself well enough to know he needed to know as much as possible about something or someone in order to satisfy his curiosity and his driving need to do the right thing. However, that didn't mean he wasn't often trying to please people, and it was the conflict between those two drives that sometimes kept him awake at night.

So when Margaret rushed over to the table, he was afraid that she had found out about Judith before he could tell her and was angry at him. He was preparing to apologize, but not back down. But as she got closer, he realized Margaret wasn't angry. She was crying.

"What's wrong?" Tanner asked, standing so quickly he almost tipped over his drink, catching it before it spilled.

As Margaret stood staring at him, all the fears he ever had about doing the wrong thing flooded over him and he felt as if he would faint, only vaguely recognizing that she probably wouldn't be crying if he had done something wrong.

Tanner watched Margaret's face change to worry as she realized he didn't know what had happened.

"You don't know, do you?"

"Know what?"

Margaret reached over and pushed Tanner back in his seat, and then gently holding his hand, she leaned in and whispered, "Marshall is dead."

49

# Eleven

An emergency meeting of the Town Council took place within hours of the news. Margaret arranged it, practically dragging Tanner out of the restaurant and taking him with her as she made phone calls to the other three Town Council members.

As they arrived, Margaret hugged each one as they came through the door, whether they wanted it or not, and led them to where she wanted them to sit. Despite her previous tears, Margaret was in her element. To Tanner, it seemed that the fact that the man they had all known and respected had died was now simply an item on Margaret's agenda.

They were meeting in the Council room at City Hall, tucked beside the larger room where they held Town Hall meetings. The entire building was abuzz. Tanner thought it literally sounded like a giant beehive, and he struggled to not get pulled into the emotional chaos that swirled through the air.

Groups of people were standing in the halls crying, while others rushed from room to room carrying stacks of papers. Tanner wondered if anyone knew what they were doing. Without Marshall, would anyone know what to do?

Yes, Marshall had retired, leaving Margaret, as head of the Town Council, as interim mayor. But everyone knew that once Marshall returned from vacation, he'd act as a consultant to make sure the transition ran smoothly. Everyone also knew that Marshall would help get Judith officially elected mayor at the next election.

Watching Margaret in action, Tanner realized something he hadn't noticed before. He should have, but he had been too busy trying to fit in to actually take in the fact that Margaret was probably the reason every one of them was there.

Of course, he was on the Council because of Margaret, but so was Colin Parker, a slim, well-dressed man who always looked as if he stepped out of a fashion magazine. Tanner considered Colin an opinionated know-it-all and always tried to sit far away from him, not wanting to be part of his ongoing commentary. He tried not to let on how much he disliked the man and he wondered why Margaret had chosen him as a Council member. Maybe because, as the owner of a large real estate office, he had connections.

Barbara Green arrived next. She had approached Tanner when he first joined the Council about hiring him, but in the end had stayed with the accountant she had for years. He knew Barbara owned a nursery in town and employed a crew of landscapers who tended to many of the lawns and gardens in Spring Falls.

The last person to arrive was Walter Lane. Walt owned a bookstore in town, with a small cafe attached to it. He was one reason Tanner had wanted to join Judith's team and get to know Judith, because it was Walt who had recently hired him as his accountant, and Tanner had already noticed a few discrepancies and wasn't sure what to do about them. Walt had warned him he would find problems, and he hoped Tanner could help him determine what he could do to fix them.

Observing Margaret as she settled everyone into their seats, Tanner contemplated the similarities between Margaret and Judith. Although Margaret didn't have Judith's flaming red hair, she was tall and imposing and controlled the room wherever she went. Perhaps Margaret thought of Judith as a rival? But why?

Although Tanner was terrible with ages, he thought Margaret and Judith might be around the same age. He knew Margaret had traveled the world, but she had grown up in Spring Falls. Maybe the two of them went to school together. It was details like that which would make him lose sleep over nothing. Things that probably weren't important had to fit together in his head. To Tanner, life was a gigantic puzzle, and he had to solve it.

He couldn't help himself. Watching each person enter the room, he noticed how they behaved. Were they sad Marshall was gone, or relieved? Or perhaps they were all even better than him at hiding their true feelings. Because he was secretly glad that Marshall had died. It solved a problem for him, or at least he hoped it did. Glancing over at Walt, he winced, hoping it didn't show. When Walt looked back at him, something passed between them. *Yes,* Tanner thought. H*e is secretly glad too. But was it for the same reason?*

Margaret stood and waited until they all gave her their full attention before speaking. After expressing her deep sorrow over Marshall's passing and asking them all to bow their heads in silence for a moment, she got down to business.

"We will need to get another Town Council member. As acting mayor, I am not counted as a member, and we need five people."

Everyone knew she also meant that she would be more than the acting mayor, but no one was going to mention that. Besides, Tanner knew that Margaret's term would have been up anyway and they would need to replace her then.

Although it was never officially stated, the Town Council had a plan in place which had kept Margaret, Barbara, Colin, and Walt on the Council for years.

John Rayburn had been the fifth Council member until he retired last year and Tanner was elected to fill his seat. Tanner thought it was only a matter of time until more Council members retired. He was the youngest one there, starting a new generation of members chosen by Margaret.

Because the by-laws stated that Council members could serve three terms, each four years long, and then they would have to take two years off before they could run again, Marshall had devised a two-part work around.

First, during their two-year absence, they were hired as consultants. And second, they would choose someone and then help them get elected. However, that person would agree to only serve one term. That enabled them to return to the Council after their two-year hiatus was up.

Somehow they had set it up so they would only have to wait those two years, while another member took their two years off. It was a brilliant strategy. Tanner was that replacement this time.

However, they hadn't counted on Marshall dying, catapulting Margaret into the position of mayor. Which meant he could stay on the Council—if he fit in. Tanner wasn't sure if either of those factors was going to be true in three years. He'd wait and see.

Glancing around the room, Tanner thought perhaps no one was sad that Marshall had died. For sure, Margaret, although putting on a righteous act of being distressed about Marshall's death, was happy about it.

To be fair, perhaps Margaret wasn't happy that Marshall had died, but she was definitely happy about the opportunities that Marshall's death brought her. She was acting as the mayor now. And Tanner was sure she couldn't wait to get started on whatever agenda she had, one Tanner was sure that she had been planning for years.

# Twelve

Like Tanner, Barbara Green watched Margaret guide the Council through the decisions they needed to make and what they had to do. She was doing it effectively and with purpose, as she had for years.

But today, despite her professed sadness over Marshall's death, there was a spark of happiness that flared up from time to time. Margaret quickly tamped it down, probably hoping no one noticed. But Barbara did.

Barbara had known and observed Margaret for too long to be fooled. She knew this was the moment Margaret had been waiting for since she had become part of the Town Council over thirty years before.

It was Marshall who had chosen Margaret and helped her get elected. From then on it was Margaret, with Marshall's blessing, who decided who to put onto the Council. Slowly, but efficiently, the two of them weeded out the old Council members.

Margaret had convinced Barbara to come onto the Council next, and then Colin, John, and Walt. It didn't take long before the five of them were the Town Council that everyone knew ran the town. And there was no one left that Marshall and Margaret hadn't chosen.

Sometimes other Council members referred to the two of them as the M&M's. But even though Margaret was the major factor in choosing who would be on the Council throughout the years, she didn't run the Council. Marshall did. Only now that Marshall was dead did the Council become completely Margaret's.

Barbara knew that most people didn't realize how much power the Town Council had along with the Mayor. At least in Spring Falls. Marshall was the king. And now Margaret was the queen.

*It might be time to leave,* Barbara thought. It would be so much easier than speaking up and telling people what she knew. Sometimes she lay awake for hours at night wondering if she should do something. Until a few months ago, it had been easier to ignore what was happening. Then one of her crew shared what was happening to her family, and it became personal.

When it had begun so many years ago, they had approached her to take part in these things. She had said no. And they had agreed that as long as she turned a blind eye to what they were doing, she could remain on the Council. And since she had loved being on the Council, she had said yes. She enjoyed being at the center of everything that was happening, but not responsible for it.

Plus, over the years, because of the Council, she had never had to advertise her business. People knew her from the Council, and that notoriety and power, plus referrals, easily grew her business. She was successful without their schemes. But as the years went by, she found it harder and harder to ignore what they were doing.

Their schemes were like an invasive plant in the garden. Eventually, it takes over and chokes out all the beauty and goodness. She told herself that she should be proud of herself for at least having the strength to not participate. But she never had the strength or courage to stop it. Now she wondered if she was ready. There may not be a better time.

Barbara was fairly sure that Margaret and the rest of them knew she was getting close to blowing—as her son might say—and they would be happy to see her drop out of the Council so they could get someone who was more of a player than she was.

Looking across the table at Tanner, who always sat far away from the blow-hard Colin, she thought the Council believed Tanner to be apathetic enough to look the other way. But she wasn't so sure about that. She was watching him. If he took a stand, she'd fire her current accountant and hire him. Perhaps then they could take on the mess together.

For now, though, all she wanted to do was go home and sit in the greenhouse she had built off her home. Within her greenhouse and with her precious orchids, she could pretend—until she almost believed it—that the world was a beautiful place.

Rocking in her chair, her cat twisting around her feet and strolling through the aisles as if she owned the world, Barbara would talk to her flowers. They knew all her secrets, including the ones that kept her up at night. But they'd never tell.

*Yes, it was probably time to leave the Council.* But first, she had to stay and help plan Marshall's funeral and then assist them in quickly finding someone else to become part of the Town Council. However, listening to Margaret and her plans, she yearned to go home to her cat and her orchids. Perhaps if everyone just said yes to Margaret, then the meeting would be over.

As she pretended to listen, Barbara thought about how much she had come to hate being in these meetings. Did she really have to stay to plan Marshall's funeral and elect someone else? Maybe she should retire now, stand up and declare her intention, and let them get two new members of the Council.

That way, she wouldn't be anywhere near what was bound to happen with Marshall dead. Margaret might be able to handle it. Of course, Margaret thought she could, but Barbara wasn't so sure. Although Margaret obviously didn't believe it, it was pure bad luck for her that Marshall had fallen down the stairs and died. Who died falling down the stairs, anyway? It was an omen. Yes, it was time to get out before it was too late.

Catching Tanner's eye, she smiled at him. Barbara knew that Margaret and Marshall selected Tanner as John Rayburn's replacement last year because he seemed like a nice but somewhat insecure and naïve individual. But Barbara thought Tanner was a quick study, and he'd learn fast. She hoped he didn't learn from all the people who bent the rules or made up new ones to suit them.

Perhaps she should take him under her wing and let him in on what she knew. But that put him in danger. Or her, if he told. She needed to find out what kind of man he was before she opened that door.

"So we are agreed?" Margaret was saying. Although Barbara did not know what they were agreeing to, she answered, "Aye." What difference would it make now if it wasn't something she wanted or believed in? It was what she had been doing for years anyway.

*Yes*, Barbara thought. *I am going to announce my retirement. I'm too old and tired to continue with this.*

As they stood, Barbara caught Margaret looking at her, and she hoped Margaret couldn't read minds because she doubted Margaret would like what she was thinking.

And then, surprising even herself, she said, "I'm announcing my retirement. This is a good time."

The gasp around the room told her no one had expected her to say that. Margaret glared, Colin smirked, and Walt looked away, but Tanner smiled as if he understood. Yes, Barbara thought, I need to talk to him. Before it's too late.

# Thirteen

Margaret watched Barbara walk out of the room, half wishing she had a brick she could hurl at her. How dare she do this now? Didn't she have enough on her plate to deal with without having to come up with another Council member?

But then Margaret realized that meant she no longer had to deal with someone who got all the glory from being a Council member but refused to take part completely. Barbara's usefulness had been an information source. Barbara's landscaping business serviced almost everyone who was anyone in town. Her landscapers were invisible. People didn't notice service workers, so they'd hear things, tell Barbara, and then Barbara would relay what she heard to the Council.

Of course, Barbara thought that the fact that she did nothing with what she knew and just passed it on made her innocent. It didn't. *Perhaps I'll have to remind her of that fact,* Margaret thought.

Tanner had followed Barbara out of the room, but not before asking if there was anything he could do. *That one could go far,*

Margaret thought. *He is supportive of everyone, even though he's quiet and doesn't seem to want to stand out.*

But not standing out was okay with Margaret. She was the one who was supposed to stand out. As long as Tanner continued to do as he was told, he would fit in well with her future plans for the Council.

As she watched Barbara and Tanner leave, Margaret decided it was going to all work out in her favor. There were a few people in town who kept demanding more in return for what they did for her. Making them part of the Town Council might be the perfect solution.

Margaret signaled for Colin and Walt to stay behind. Not for the same reasons. She needed to ask for Colin's advice. But she wanted to talk to Walt because of a recent shift in his behavior. Something was bothering him, and that wasn't a good thing. She thought a private lunch with Walt might shed light on what was unsettling him.

Colin was easily influenced, but that was primarily because Margaret understood precisely how to steer him in ways that kept him happy. His importance to their plans couldn't be overstated. Unlike Barbara, whose worth lay mostly in her connections and knowledge, Colin also collected information, but he was not averse to rolling up his sleeves and immersing himself in the nitty-gritty of what needed to be done.

Margaret saw Colin as a reliable figure—someone she could trust to carry out tasks diligently. Of everyone on the Council, he was the most conscientious. Although he was often so high and mighty about it, she sometimes wanted to slap him.

"Two people?" Colin huffed.

"We already had someone in mind since I would be leaving anyway, but yes, we need someone else. Perhaps this isn't a bad thing. Let's look for someone who will be useful to our plans."

"Do you have any ideas?" Walt asked, thinking that he wished he had stood up and retired like Barbara just did. It might have been accepted. After all, Barbara was only a few years older than him. They were at an age where people expected them to retire. He could go home and put all this behind him. Just concentrate on his bookstore. Have time to read more books. Escape from the nastiness of life.

But now it was too late. He didn't think quickly enough. It was the story of his life. Always a beat behind. He was stuck in something he should have gotten out of a long time ago. But he had thought it was his duty to stay. To be loyal. However, recently, he had been asking himself to what was he loyal? And why?

Now that Marshall was dead, it could mean a new life for him. Perhaps now he could be loyal to something more than Marshall and Margaret's plan. A plan everyone on the Council had agreed with.

But how was he going to start a new life while still a member of the Council? Tanner might be able to help, but would he be willing to take the risk?

What Walt really wanted to do was walk away from it all. It was tempting. Just leave everything behind. Walk away. But he knew that wasn't possible. And although he deeply grieved for his wife, who had passed away years before, he was also glad that she hadn't lived long enough to see the hole he had dug for himself and could probably never get out of.

She had warned him. Told him that every decision he made would affect his future self—their future. But each decision to say yes to a scheme, or turn away and pretend to not see what was happening, seemed so innocent at the time. Who did it hurt? But even then, he knew he was lying to himself. And now it was too late. Not for the first time, Walt was glad he didn't have children. He wouldn't have been a good role model for them.

Margaret smiled at the two men in front of her. She understood them both. They knew who was in charge, and they both had agreed to the plan long ago. Although she sensed Walt's recent reluctance, it was something she could handle. If necessary, she would remind him of what he had done with the rest of them. She didn't think it would be necessary.

"I have a few people in mind," Margaret answered. "I'll need your help in approaching them, and then bringing them on board. We'll have to act fast. There are people in town who might see this as an opportunity to make changes on the board or even run for mayor. You both know we can't have that."

Margaret didn't need to say who those people were who might run for the Council or mayor. They all knew that one of them was Judith Zoe. And they all knew that was a problem. Judith was well known and loved in Spring Falls. If Judith decided things needed to change, she wouldn't hesitate to fight for that change and there were many people who would back her.

Everything they had put together through the years might unravel. Margaret would rather die than have that happen.

What Margaret didn't know was how quickly they would need to act. She didn't know that Tanner had already started the process to involve Judith. A process that would lead Judith to discover what they had done. And even though Margaret thought she knew the men standing in front of her, she hadn't counted on Walt's guilty conscious working overtime and Colin's ambition.

If she had, she might have tried to stop them both that day. Instead, she made an appointment for lunch with Walt, and sent Colin to talk to her choice of people about joining the Council. Knowing them, it would make their day.

As for Margaret, her days were about to get worse.

# Fourteen

Judith wasn't actually sure where she was going when she walked out the door of her office. She only knew she couldn't sit around waiting to find answers, she needed to go get them now. But from where? Booker wasn't talking, or at least he wasn't talking to the Ruby Sisters. Maybe she could get him to talk to her.

But first, she walked, because sometimes answers appeared out of nowhere when she walked. Maybe it would work this time. As always, when she was trying to figure something out, she talked to herself and her red hair would seem to flare. Of course, that wasn't possible. But that's what it always looked like to people who saw her striding down the street.

And today, everyone saw her. Because as the news spread of their beloved mayor's death, people had stopped what they were doing and stared out their windows. If it wasn't so cold and windy, the streets would have been filled with people milling around trying to understand how this could have happened.

Instead, they all breathed a small sigh of relief as they watched Judith. No one liked to be on the end of Judith's relentless drive to get to the bottom of things, but they all respected and trusted her.

They knew Judith would find out how Marshall had died. And if there was something suspicious about it, she would find out the truth.

As she walked, Judith thought about her uneasiness over the past few months. She had often talked about it to Bruce, trying to make sense of it. There was something happening, and to Judith, it felt as if it was dangerous to Spring Falls. However, the whole idea of it had seemed so ludicrous, she kept telling herself she was imagining it. Worrying over nothing.

But now that Marshall had died, she wondered if that was what she had felt. Some kind of premonition. But, as distressing as it was that Marshall was dead, it wasn't the end of the world. After all, he was retiring anyway. Plans were already in place. Margaret would run for mayor in the fall.

All that had changed was that Margaret would become interim mayor now. In fact, Judith knew it would suit Margaret far better to have it happen this way. Margaret was a shoo-in for becoming mayor. Knowing Margaret, Judith was sure that she had already picked her replacement.

And she did know Margaret. They had grown up in Spring Falls together. Margaret was a few years ahead of her in high school and already in charge. Margaret had run for Student Council president and won hands down. Judith had admired her then. She still did.

In some ways, she had patterned herself after Margaret. Take charge. Get things done. They were both like that. The fundamental difference, as far as Judith could tell, is that Margaret loved to be in the spotlight and she did not.

And both were often in the spotlight. The difference was that Margaret made it happen for herself, and for Judith, it only happened because of her work with so many businesses in town. Plus, everyone knew she couldn't stop herself from fixing things that were broken. Which, in Judith's world, meant when something was going on that she thought was wrong.

So although she and Margaret knew each other, they never became friends. Judith thought it might be because Margaret didn't want to share the spotlight, and Judith knew on her part it was because Margaret was too much about Margaret. It set her teeth on edge.

Still, Judith had to be happy for Margaret. She was finally getting what she probably set out to get long ago. She would be the mayor of Spring Falls. The only thing Judith didn't understand was why. It was a small town. Why not go to a big city and take it over? Maybe Margaret preferred to be a big fish in a small pond, rather than just another person trying to get ahead in a big city.

*That's probably it,* Judith thought to herself. But if all she had been worried about was Marshall's death, then why did she still feel that uneasiness? In fact, now the uneasiness was worse. So, as much as she wanted her uneasiness to have been solved by Marshall dying, Judith knew it wasn't. Something was still very wrong in Spring Falls.

With that thought, Judith quickened her steps, and without her knowing that it happened, her hair flared. A couple who were in town to see their daughter in college walked by Judith and noticed the flare. And then looked back at the retreating figure, thought that a beam of sunlight must have struck her hair. Otherwise, what they had seen would be impossible.

They glanced up at the sky and wondered where the sun could have come from. Dark clouds hung heavy above them. They looked at each other, shook their heads, and decided to just accept that it had happened without knowing what it meant. People who lived in town knew exactly what it meant. Judith Zoe was on the warpath, probably over the mayor's death.

Judith was so familiar with the streets that she didn't pay attention to her surroundings. She only realized she was at the driveway of the Ruby House when her phone rang. Glancing at the screen, she saw it was Tanner. For a minute, she hesitated.

She didn't want to conduct business right now. But then she remembered Tanner was on the Town Council, and he might have news.

"Could we meet right now?" Tanner asked, sounding slightly breathless. But perhaps that was because he was whispering.

When Judith hesitated, he added, "It's important. And private."

Judith turned and started back to her office. It was the most private place she knew.

"My office."

"Be there in a few," Tanner whispered and hung up.

But when he arrived, he wasn't alone. Barbara Green was with him. Of course, Judith knew who Barbara was. Who didn't? It was Barbara's landscape company that took care of her yard and garden. In fact, all the Ruby Sisters used her services.

When Judith went to Barbara's nursery to buy plants, Barbara would often talk to people and help them decide what would work best in their gardens. But other than their brief conversations at the nursery and sometimes at Town Hall meetings, Judith didn't know Barbara well.

Now, looking at the two of them standing in her office, she realized she felt afraid. Something was about to change, and she wasn't so sure that she was ready. Perhaps Tanner and Barbara were there to ask her to become a member of the Town Council. She already knew her answer. No. It would be a conflict of interest.

But once she had them seated in her office, the blind behind her closed, the lights low so the room felt comfortable and safe, she thought she might be wrong about why they were there. The hair on the back of her neck stood up as Tanner leaned forward and asked her if what they told her would remain private.

"Only if it doesn't affect other people negatively."

Barbara whispered something to Tanner, her face pale. Judith thought she had aged ten years since she had seen her last week at the coffee shop.

Something had changed. And it couldn't just be Marshall's death. Could it?

# Fifteen

Emma returned from her run wet, cold, and confused. She had gone to the Green Zone, where no construction would ever take place, and saw a clearing in the woods. And equipment.

Someone hid it well. Unless you were on foot, you'd miss it because a band of trees surrounded it. Despite that, she had seen it, and she knew it was something she wasn't supposed to see. It was so unexpected that she stopped and stared, wishing she was mistaken but angry because she knew she wasn't. To Emma, who loved this forest, what she was looking at was a travesty. She had stood there, not moving, not realizing she was crying.

In a vast swath of land, everything was gone. Trees and the underbrush were completely gone. And instead there was a row of partially built houses. So either something was going on that shouldn't be going on, or she was in the wrong place. She didn't think she was. So she was angry, sad, furious, and disgusted.

But just to make sure she had come to the right place, and that she wasn't losing her mind, she took a few pictures on her phone, thinking she would show Judith. Judith would know what to do. Tucking her phone back into her fanny pack, she turned away from the devastation, but not before apologizing to what was no longer there. Although she hadn't done it, perhaps she should have noticed something was wrong before this terrible thing happened.

But it was too late and too cold to be standing around, just staring at the ruin of the forest. Besides, maybe she shouldn't be there. Something about the whole thing made her nervous. She kept expecting someone to pop out of nowhere and yell at her.

Thirty minutes later, when Veronica came out of the kitchen where she had been making Emma a batch of pancakes, she saw her daughter standing on the mat in the coatroom, still dripping water, and looking upset.

"What's wrong? Did you hurt yourself?"

Emma looked up and realized she was still in her wet coat and shoes. "Oh, sorry," she said as she slipped out of both, hanging up her coat and putting her shoes on the mat. "Just thinking."

"Well, go get out of your wet clothes, and come eat the pancakes I made you. Maybe you can tell me what you were thinking about."

Minutes later, Emma was at the table, digging into her stack of pancakes, each bite swirled first in the real maple syrup they could now afford. *Thanks to Daniel*, Emma thought.

She still couldn't believe her good fortune. Her mom had found a half brother, and now she had an uncle she adored. Or more accurately, Daniel had found them because somehow the universe had brought him to town with April's son, Robert.

And then it turned out that Daniel had seen Cindy when he was ten years old and fallen in love with her. And her grandmother had been friends with Cindy when they met at Daniel's father, Cedric's, art studio. No one would believe that story, except that it had happened in her life.

Until Daniel found them, Emma didn't really believe in the interconnectedness of all things. But too many things had happened in the past year that couldn't be explained any other way.

And now Daniel was living with Cindy, who was helping her become the artist she had always dreamed of becoming. Just like her grandmother and mother, who never had the chance. So she wasn't just wanting that dream for herself, it was to honor them, too.

Between art, dance, a new acting class Marsha had begun, her mom not stressed anymore, the new friends she had made, everything about her life was perfect now. She didn't want to think that something could spoil it. She could ignore what she saw. *Someone else could take care of it. But what if they didn't? She'd feel guilty forever about doing nothing.*

All she could hope for was that she was wrong. But she would soon discover that she wasn't. And what she had seen was only the tip of the iceberg. It was what Judith had sensed long ago. A danger faced the town that would—as always when evil is revealed—change the people of Spring Falls forever.

So after the pancakes were eaten and the dishes were washed, instead of setting out her homeschooling lessons for the day, her mother sat down, took her daughter's hands in hers, and asked, "Tell me what happened."

After all that they had been through together, Emma knew that she could trust her mother, so she answered, "I ran to a section of the Green Zone, or I think I was there, and I saw something that shouldn't be there. Or at least I don't think it should."

Seeing her mother's puzzled face, she took out her phone and showed her the pictures she had taken.

It was only when she saw her mother's face turn pale that Emma accepted she was right. Something terrible had happened.

"We need to tell Judith. We'll go after my lunch shift at ParaTi's. Instead of your regular homework, can you look up everything you can find about the Green Zone?"

Emma nodded, grateful that her mother didn't just push her worries aside and was willing to find out the truth with her. But then, if she was honest with herself, which she was trying to be, her mother had always been on her side.

# Sixteen

arsha and April had just finished lunch in the 2nd floor kitchen of the Ruby House. April was downstairs in her office preparing for her meeting with a new client. Marsha was debating with herself what to do with her afternoon. She had work to do, but she was stalling, as she often did. She had so many projects in the works, she didn't know where to start.

She was trying to decide what task was the most important and waiting for inspiration to strike, gazing out the front window towards town, when she saw Judith standing at the end of their driveway.

*Well, that's unexpected,* she thought. *But lovely. A good way to spend some time this afternoon. Besides, Judith wouldn't be here if there wasn't something important going on.*

If it had been summer, Marsha wouldn't have been able to see Judith. The large maple tree in the front yard would have blocked her view. But now its bare limbs were outlined against the dark sky with a dusting of snow, and it was easy to see into town. It made for a beautiful scene. If she were an artist, she'd paint it.

Marsha thought that there was something amazing about trees. Especially this one. Sometimes she'd walk to the tree and talk things over with it. Or just hug it, thinking nothing. And somehow the tree always made everything better. It didn't matter the season. It was always there for her. Actually, it was there for anyone who noticed, and even those who did not.

Marsha thought her favorite season might be winter, when the tree limbs were bare. Then she could see the entire outline of the tree. Every tree's structure was similar to its species but unique to itself, depending on what happened as it was growing. *Like people,* Marsha thought.

She imagined this tree having been present when the town had only a few people living in what became Spring Falls. Who planted it? Or did it plant itself? What had it seen and experienced? How had that affected what it looked like now?

Did the tree weep for man's inhumanity to man? Did it mourn for the cruelty, both intentional and unintentional, that humans did to each other and other beings? Did it despair as it watched the greed that was destroying the world?

All of those thoughts passed through her mind as she waited for Judith to walk up her driveway, and it didn't help her mood. She really didn't want to think about the mess humans were making in the world. She just wanted to teach students how to dance and do theater. What they did with it didn't matter. She knew that being in those classes opened both their minds and bodies to possibilities. She wanted to help them see the world as a beautiful place. If they took care of it.

*Thank God for Spring Falls*, Marsha thought. At least the people here care. She was a huge supporter of the Green Zone. Perhaps Spring Falls could be a beacon of light to other small towns.

But Judith was standing at the end of their drive. Why was she there? Did it have something to do with Marshall's death? She and

April had heard about it the same way everyone else in Spring Falls had.

Within hours, they both had received multiple texts. However, the facts were sparse. The conjecture of how and why ran wild. Maybe Judith knew more, and she was coming over to discuss it with them.

As she watched Judith at the end of the drive, Marsha saw Judith answer her phone, pause, and abruptly turn away. Marsha, a student of body language, didn't need to see Judith's red hair flaming to know that something had happened. And she was betting it wasn't a good thing.

*Maybe I'll just go back to bed*, Marsha thought.

But then the tree shivered as a gust of wind swept through, and she reminded herself that, like the tree, she was strong and capable, and there was no turning away from whatever was happening.,

Downstairs in April's office, April's client couldn't stop talking about Marshall's death. April kept trying to rein him back in, discuss the remodeling of his office building, but he remained distracted by the news.

Finally, she gave in and asked him if he had known Marshall well.

"I thought I did," the client replied. "But lately he seemed more withdrawn."

"Was he unhappy?"

"No, actually, I think he was happier. But over what? I asked him one time, and he just smiled at me and said something inane like, 'things are going well."

"Did you ask him what things?"

"I did."

April could imagine that her client did. He was the curious sort. Very hands on. If they ever got around to remodeling his office, she knew he would be the kind of client who had to know everything. How much did something cost? Why did she use that? So now, she could imagine that he didn't let Marshall get away with not answering.

"And, what did he say?"

"It was the strangest thing. He wouldn't tell me. Just said I'd find out soon enough."

"I don't imagine that sat well with you."

"It didn't. But what could I do?"

"And now he's dead."

"And now he's dead, her client repeated. And I'll never find out what he meant."

Of course, he was wrong. They'd all find out why Marshall was happy. And that would be when they realized they never really knew Marshall Ferguson.

# Seventeen

Convinced that Marshall's death wasn't an accident, Booker stepped up the investigation. He sent his team to talk to the neighbors and check nearby security cameras for any useful footage.

Marshall's own security system had been disconnected, with its memory wiped clean. Under normal circumstances, this would make no sense, especially if Marshall was just leaving for a vacation. But once the realtor told Booker the house was for sale, he understood. Marshall had no intention of returning to Spring Falls, and he wanted nothing left behind.

Booker wondered if perhaps that was where Marshall's computer had gone. Perhaps he had sent it on to wherever he was going. But he doubted it. Marshall and his computer were bound at the hip. He'd have it with him whether he was going on a vacation or was leaving town for good. Someone had taken it, and the only reason they would do that was because there was something on the computer that they didn't want anyone to see.

While his team fanned out across the neighborhood, Booker planned to approach the Town Council members, the closest semblance of family that Marshall had.

Margaret picked up immediately. Not bothering to say hello, she blurted out, "I figured I'd hear from you sooner or later."

"I thought I would give you a head's up that I'm headed to your office."

"Come ahead, but I'm in Marshall's office at the Town Hall."

"Give me ten."

While she waited, Margaret went to the restroom. Washing her hands, she checked herself in the mirror, tilting her head at her reflection, and judged it adequate for the conversation with Booker. She was as put together as she always was, but she had tousled her carefully dyed blond hair just enough to look as if she was in disarray over Marshall's death.

She wondered if she should cry a little to redden her eyes, but decided that was overkill, and Booker would never buy it, anyway.

The coffee in the Town Hall was bland, almost tasteless, so Margaret sent her assistant to fetch better quality coffee from a nearby cafe. As she thought of the many hours she'd be spending in the Town Hall in the future, she toyed with the idea of investing in an espresso machine.

It would improve not only the quality of the coffee but also the office ambiance. In fact, she had grand plans to revamp the mayor's office. These ideas had been brewing for a long time, but now she had the opportunity to implement them. However, she would bide her time until her position as the mayor was officially announced.

The smell of fresh coffee was the first thing Booker noticed. It was a silent testament to Margaret's usual attention to detail. A reminder not to underestimate her. Booker knew that Margaret and Marshall had been the force behind what some people saw as the ruthless efficiency of the Town Council.

Margaret met him with a carefully neutral expression, her icy blue eyes betraying nothing. If she felt grief, it didn't show. He didn't expect her to, which is probably why she didn't pretend to. Marshall and Margaret might have been friends, but Margaret had been waiting for this moment for years.

Instead of hiding her grief, Booker assumed Margaret was hiding her happiness. Her moment would come sooner now. There was no doubt she would remain mayor now that Marshall had died. No one was going to want to run against her now. It would feel like disrespect for Marshall.

"Sheriff," she greeted him, gesturing to the coffee and pastries on the table. "Help yourself."

"Thank you," Booker replied. His eyes met hers as he took a cautious sip of coffee, instantly recognizing the quality. He raised an eyebrow in a silent question.

"A little comfort in these difficult times," Margaret explained, a hint of a smile on her lips. The warmth didn't quite reach her eyes, adding an edge to her words that Booker filed away to think about later.

"Difficult times indeed," Booker agreed, setting his coffee down. "Let's cut to the chase, Margaret. When was the last time you saw Marshall?"

Margaret's gaze didn't waver, but Booker noticed the slightest pause before she answered, "Last week, at the Town Council meeting. I am assuming you mean other than Saturday night when everyone saw Marshall."

"And there was nothing unusual about his demeanor? Nothing that indicated he had plans to leave town for good? Even on Saturday night? He didn't give away his plans?" Booker probed.

Margaret shook her head, her blond hair shimmering under the room's florescent lighting. Booker suspected she would change out those lights to be more flattering the first chance she got.

"Marshall always kept his cards close to his chest," she replied. "I can't say I knew much about his personal affairs. Why would he be leaving town for good? His plans were to come back after his vacation and help me run for mayor.

"Of course he was happy at the party. Who could blame him? Forty years with a spotless record. Not many people can say that."

Booker studied her for a moment longer before nodding and taking a thoughtful sip of his coffee. This was just the beginning of a long investigation, and he intended to follow every lead, however minor it may seem. This wasn't anything other than a courtesy meeting.

He planned to talk to everyone on the Council. Casually at first, but he would watch to see what they did in Marshall's absence.

After asking a few more questions, Booker said he'd get back to her later. But first he wanted to speak to all the Council members. They shook hands—on the surface friendly and on the same side.

But for Booker's part, he was more sure than ever that Marshall's death had not been an accident. Perhaps he wasn't the beloved mayor everyone had thought he was. And Margaret didn't seem surprised at the mention that Marshall hadn't planned to return from vacation. What else did she know?

Margaret watched Booker's departure with a gaze as sharp as a hawk, her mind churning with plans and predictions.

And so, the two danced around each other, one searching for answers, and the other holding her secrets close. The journey to uncover the truth of Marshall's demise had just begun, and in the quiet town of Spring Falls, their dance would determine the fate of many.

# Eighteen

"Barbara, are you alright?" Judith asked. Neither Tanner nor Barbara had said anything yet, and Judith was getting impatient. What was going on? Tanner looked worried, but Barbara seemed scared. Barbara only nodded in response, clutching the cup of coffee that Nancy had brought her as if it were a lifeline.

Tanner put a comforting hand on Barbara's shoulder, sharing a brief, intense look with Judith. He had brought Barbara here, and even though he knew he wasn't responsible for the distress Barbara was in, he felt terrible anyway.

He liked Barbara, even though he suspected she was part of what was going on in the Town Council. Maybe she had not taken part, but she had also said nothing. Perhaps she was like Walt, who had come to him earlier and hinted to him what the Town Council was doing. Tanner still wasn't sure he could trust Walt, but for some reason, he was more likely to give Barbara the benefit of the doubt. Maybe because she reminded him of his mother.

Like his mother, Barbara had always struck him as mischievous, enjoying the small prank or unexpected comment. Yet, sometimes his mother would fall into a deep depression, and he had to wait her out. Now, what Barbara was doing felt the same to him. Withdrawn, depressed.

Which was why even though they had come to Judith to get her advice, neither of them were speaking, which just increased the tension in the room that was gathering around Barbara like a storm cloud.

When Barbara didn't answer, Judith decided to wait them both out. Barbara stuck in her fear, Tanner in his worry. They were in her office for a reason. Eventually, they'd tell her what was going on. Getting mad or upset wouldn't work.

Instead, Judith leaned back in her chair and sipped her coffee, looking as if she had all the time in the world, while feeling like flinging something to break them both out of their silent spell. They had obviously come to tell her something, but what?

Tanner had a crease between his brows that hadn't been there before. Judith watched as he murmured something in Barbara's ear, trying to provide some comfort, but it seemed to have little effect. Barbara remained silent, obviously struggling with what to say.

Judith understood that Marshall's death was a blow to the entire community, and probably even more to the Council members. Marshall was a pillar in Spring Falls, a constant presence that no one had ever thought would be suddenly taken away.

But this, Judith thought, this is something else. She could feel a deep unease that seemed to radiate off Barbara like a dark cloud.

"Barbara, if you need to talk, I'm listening," Judith offered again, the words hanging heavy in the quiet room. Barbara offered her a small, sad smile, but still said nothing.

Barbara wanted to speak, but she didn't know where to start. She wanted to tell Judith everything. She was tired of carrying the burden of what she had done. With Tanners' help, she had gotten herself as far as Judith's office, where she had meant to blurt out everything. But fear and guilt kept her from speaking.

She kept asking herself what would happen once she told what she knew? What would happen when she told them of the financial transactions that had been going on for years, right under the town's nose? What would happen when Judith learned that Marshall, the town's beloved mayor, had been accepting bribes for years?

What would happen when she told Judith that members of the Town Council had participated in this deception? Or, in her case, looked away. She wanted to believe that she was innocent, but she knew once she told Judith, she would have to admit that she wasn't. None of them were.

Even more worrying was that she knew someone had redirected Town Council funds to an offshore account just days before Marshall's death. Did Marshall move them? Is that why he was pretending to go on a vacation, but was really leaving town? Barbara was worried that someone else was involved. Someone who had been aware of Marshall's misdeeds and had taken advantage of the situation.

But if someone else was involved, who was it, and for how long had they been? And, most importantly, was Marshall's death truly an accident, or did someone take action to cover up what had been happening? These were the burdens Barbara bore in silence, the secrets that aged her and painted worry in her once bright eyes.

At the same time, Barbara thought that now that Marshall was dead, it was the perfect time to come clean. Perhaps work out some kind of deal. It was why she had come to Tanner. She knew he had spoken to Judith. She knew Walt had already tried to point Tanner in the right direction without incriminating himself.

So eventually the truth would come out, and it would be better for her if she told first. But despite Tanner's reassuring presence and Judith's apparent concern for her, she couldn't stop asking herself what would happen when she told.

Barbara knew that when she revealed what she knew, they would charge her as guilty the same as everyone else involved. She had known what was going on for years. Still, she couldn't stop thinking that there might be a way she could make herself be seen as innocent. Her hesitation to speak up was driven by fear of self-incrimination and the potential fallout it could cause.

Barbara jumped when Judith put her coffee down, and glancing at Tanner, turned all her attention to her and said, "Now Barbara. Out with it."

Seeing Barbara's distress, Tanner made a decision. He'd tell what he knew, even though it wasn't much, and perhaps that would give Barbara the courage to speak up. Then maybe they could convince Walt to join them. Because even though Walt had expressed a desire to come clean about what he knew, Tanner wasn't so sure that would happen.

Taking a deep breath, he began. He didn't know much, but it was a beginning.

# Nineteen

Colin was glad it wasn't him going to lunch with Margaret. He knew the cock and bull story Margaret would feed Walt. Which was good. Walt needed to be reminded of their agreement. Walt had been acting strange lately, but he knew Margaret was aware of it and would handle it.

Instead, his mission was to recruit the two people that Margaret had decided should be on the Council. One to replace her, and one to replace that coward, Barbara.

But that wasn't what he was doing. He had gone home, made himself a drink, and settled down in his favorite chair to think things over. Margaret thought she was his boss, but she wasn't. He was his own boss, he always had been, and that would not change now. He did what she asked him to do only if it worked for him.

Sure, he let Margaret believe he was following her orders. Why not? That was part of the con he'd been playing since they made him a member of the Town Council. Making people believe what they wanted to believe was his gift. He fooled people all the time. He did what was right for him, and no one else. And since Marshall had been aware of Colin's gift, Marshall made sure what he wanted Colin to do was what Colin wanted for himself.

But even then, despite what Marshall believed, Colin only followed orders if and when he was sure it was best for him. And he was rarely confused about what he wanted. Life, and his needs, were crystal clear to him. He always had a plan, and he knew every bit of how it would work. It might have taken him longer in school to learn something, but once he did, he remembered it forever.

But right now, he wasn't sure what to do next. How could he be? Marshall was gone. His plans had to change. Life as they knew it was over. Sooner or later, their misdeeds would be discovered. Colin knew Margaret was delusional if she thought she could contain the past.

It was Marshall who had been the tactician, the one who could read every situation and know what to do. Marshall was the person who loved the crowds and the people and never faltered once his mind was made up.

Colin had never been under any illusion that Marshall had anyone's best interests in mind other than his own. But as long as what Marshall wanted served him too, Colin was happy to let Marshall lead the way and he would carefully follow. Now there was no one to follow. Because he certainly wouldn't be following Margaret.

Colin clinked the ice in his class, swirled the amber liquid, and thought through his choices. Was it time for the Town Council to publicly claim their right to do what they had done? Could they support that claim? Probably not.

*No,* Colin thought, *making public what they had done shouldn't happen. It was clear that what they had been doing was illegal.*

Could he claim he didn't know? Or should he turn them all in first and take his punishment? He could work out a deal. He wouldn't spend a long time in prison, and after that, he'd be a free and very wealthy man. He had hidden his money well.

Or should he do what Marshall had been planning to do and get out of town before anyone found out? He'd leave the country. He'd leave his closet of bespoke suits and the townhouse, furnished to perfection, behind. Forget about the life he had cultivated and dreamed about since he and Walt were in grade school together.

All he had ever wanted was to be powerful and wealthy. No one's slave or a kid to be kicked around. When Marshall tried to bully him into participation, he refused. He made his own choices. Once Marshall realized that, their working relationship improved, and they made more money together than he had thought possible..

However, Colin's wealth came from many sources. The kickbacks from Marshall's schemes were only a small part of his wealth. Most of it came from what he did on his own. That included wise investments and owning a highly successful real estate firm.

He and his team had sold more than half the houses in town. It was his knowledge of Spring Falls and the people who lived there that had provided Marshall and Margaret with what they needed to make their deals.

Plus, he had been wise in life, too. Unlike many of his colleagues, he hadn't made the mistake of falling for a woman, marrying her, and then needing to pay her off when he found another woman foolish enough to think they were the one. His romantic partners never ended up with any of his money. They were never that important to him.

His affairs, like himself, were discreet and private and controlled. He ended them when he was ready to because they no longer served him. Male or female, it made no difference to him. He had houses all over town he could use while having his affairs. Never his home. Never theirs.

Sometimes he used the knowledge he gained from those affairs to make more money. Another stream of income that wasn't part of his business dealings with Marshall or Margaret.

But all that was in the past. It all ended when Marshall fell down the stairs. And now he needed to make a plan for what to do next. What was the wisest course of action for him? Should he do Margaret's bidding? Should he confront Walt and make sure he was keeping his mouth shut? And Barbara was always a worry. Always had been. Maybe he'd have to deal with her separately.

Should he stay in town, keep his business running, but disentangle himself from the deals that Marshall had made? Looking back, he realized he probably should never have said yes to Marshall. He was plenty successful on his own. But he had said yes. Now what? Should he leave and start over? Make life simpler somewhere else? Live off his hidden wealth?

Outside, the falling snow grew thicker. It was no longer just drifting down. Through his window, Colin could see that the snow looked like someone had opened thousands of feather pillows. It was so thick that he couldn't see the trees in his yard. He could hear the snowplow coming down the street.

No one was going to do much in this storm. He had time to make his plans on how to extract himself from the other storm heading his way. Booker was no fool. He'd soon figure out what happened. And then there was Judith. She wouldn't let it go either. She was like Margaret, but on the other side. Margaret broke things. Judith fixed things. And now that the town was broken, Judith would lead the way to figuring out what happened and deciding what to do about it.

Turning to the table beside his chair, Colin grabbed the remote for his gas fireplace and switched it on. He might as well make himself comfortable. He had some work to do. Then, opening a drawer in the table, he pulled out one of his disposable phones and made a brief phone call.

"No, no one had turned in a cufflink. Yes, the room had been cleaned."

Colin shrugged. He must have lost it some place else. It wasn't important.

Pouring himself another drink from the bottle sitting beside him, Colin leaned back in his chair and started planning.

87

# Twenty

Colin was right. Margaret was wooing Walt back into the arms of the Council. But Walt was watching everything that she did and everything she said, and as if he was no longer part of the world. He was outside of himself, looking at the scene as if it had nothing to do with him.

He could see and hear Margaret, but none of it seemed real. Margaret smiling and tossing her overly styled blond hair, her blue eyes sparkling at him as if he were important to her, was like watching a movie.

When he was younger, he had fallen for Margaret's charms. Even in first grade, he had known about Margaret Williams. Everyone did. She was the high school cheerleader everyone watched at the football games. She was everywhere, her long blond hair streaming in the wind. The movie "Ten" could have been made about her.

Walt thought every boy in town probably dreamed about Margaret, no matter how old they were. But then and now, she controlled her world and made it work her way. If you were lucky enough to be part of it, she would shine her light on you. If you weren't important to her, she barely noticed you.

So when she and Marshall asked Walt to run for Town Council, it was a dream come true. It meant that he could bask a little in her light. Sometimes he felt guilty thinking that his crush on Margaret was cheating on his wife, something he would never do. But that crush had survived all those years, and remained despite his growing awareness that Margaret was not a light at all, but a dark hole that sucked people in.

Walt understood, even during those first heady years on the Council, that Margaret wasn't offering anything like respect or love. She was offering power, and he couldn't resist that then. Especially since so often he felt powerless himself.

Margaret and Marshall always seemed to know what to do. He, on the other hand, could decide nothing. Or at least it took him forever to make up his mind. So instead of resisting or speaking up, he went along with their plans. It was easier that way.

So no, he had never cheated on his wife. But he had cheated himself out of a life not consumed by what Margaret and Marshall wanted. But he had changed. And now, none of what Margaret was saying or doing was working on him. He was outside of it all.

This feeling of unreality had happened to him before. As he nursed his dying wife, he would often see the world as if he lived outside of it. Then, it was because of the pain he was feeling. Maybe that was why it was happening now. But the pain of watching his wife die and knowing he had not told her the whole truth differed from the pain he felt now.

The pain of of losing his wife had dulled, but it was always present, like a weight he could never put down. He had fallen in love with his wife the moment they met in college. Later, she would tell her friends that she fell in love with him at first sight, too. But he was sure it wasn't as intense for her as it was for him.

It didn't matter. They were in love, got married, and liked the happy-ever-after of fairy tales. They had the perfect life together.

He loved working out in the world, talking to the people who visited the bookstore about anything.

After work, he'd come home to his wife who had spent the day taking care of the house and garden, and reading about so many subjects he didn't know how she remembered them all. She'd share what she learned, they'd marvel at the world together, and he'd tell her about the people he met and what was going on in Spring Falls.

Sometimes they would take off and travel for a few days, or even a week—putting the bookstore in the capable hands of his manager—and go see the world together. They had chosen not to have kids or pets, just so they could have that kind of freedom. At the drop of a hat, they'd do whatever they wanted to do.

But as she lay in bed, holding his hand, he was looking back on what he had never told her. She thought he had made all his money running the bookstore. She had been so proud of him because he sold books—a noble profession, to her.

She said that books changed the world. Books were filled with dreams and knowledge and out-of-this-world experiences. They helped people. They had the power to make life better. And she loved that he was also helping the people of Spring Falls as a member of the Town Council.

Walt remembered how excited she was for him when he was asked to run. And when he was elected, she threw a party for him. She was the perfect wife for a member of the Council, because despite loving to spend her days alone, she knew how to work a room. Everyone loved her. He thought she genuinely loved meeting each person and learning something about them, which she never forgot.

There were times he was trying to decide about something the Council was doing that involved someone in town, and his wife would remember the perfect thing about that person and that would help resolve the situation.

What she didn't know was how much he hated himself for doing what Marshall and Margaret wanted him to do. That he would allow what his wife told him to be used by Marshall to get what he wanted. In return, they paid Walt well. But he always thought of it as hush money. Keep quiet or else.

And he had kept quiet. But as the years passed after his wife's death, he became more upset with himself. He stopped taking part in the Council's schemes, but he did nothing to stop them, either.

Until Tanner was elected. Walt saw it as an opportunity to bring to light what was going on. He tried not to think about what that would mean for his life when all that he did came to light. That's not what he wanted. He simply wanted the fraud to stop.

So now Margaret's charm was useless. And as she watched Walt and realized that he was not being taken in by what she was saying or doing, it shocked her. And scared her. How long had Walt not been under her spell? And what was she going to do about it?

# Twenty One

ParaTi's was packed. Maybe because of the snowstorm, or maybe because it was Monday. Whatever was causing it, the restaurant was overflowing. Even the benches by the door were filled with people waiting for a table, their coats open, scarves unhooked, and wet boots dripping water onto the floor.

Like her daughter, Veronica was not a fan of February. The mud, slush, and wet snow everywhere made her yearn for spring. Thankfully, Valentine's Day was over. She was also not a fan of those fake special days made up by a card company, although she supposed people sometimes needed to be reminded to tell their loved ones how much they were loved.

It was not something she needed to be reminded of. She loved her daughter with her whole heart, and it saddened her to think that Emma would only be hers for a few more years before she went out into the world on her own. And then what would happen? Would she become someone else? Veronica knew she couldn't expect the closeness they had now. So she treasured each day.

Right now, Emma was her entire world, so even though she was taking care of multiple tables at one time, her mind was occupied by what Emma had told her. That worry, along with the mess that the weather made in the restaurant, kept her from seeing the two people tucked against the wall in the back, until her friend Mary asked her to check on them for her.

Veronica had said yes, even though she was also feeling overwhelmed. Glancing at the table, she paused. She knew who they were. They had been in many times before, but usually with the entire Town Council.

Sometimes she would overhear bits of news, and she'd pass the tidbits on to Emma. They both wanted to learn as much as they could about their new home. Today, as always, Margaret was leaning forward, talking intensely. What was different this time was that Walt seemed detached and uninterested in what she was saying.

Veronica assumed that Walt and Margaret were talking about the mayor's death, and a pang of sympathy shot through her. When she had come to work, the first thing she had heard was that the mayor had died. Some freak accident. He had fallen down the stairs. *So tragic,* Veronica thought. *He never got to go on vacation, let alone enjoy years of retirement after working so hard for Spring Falls.*

Veronica thought about what Emma had told her that morning. She wondered if Walt and Margaret could shed some light on it. As she approached their table, she saw Margaret's face tighten with exasperation, and Walt's eyes plead for a distraction, as if he wished to escape the conversation.

Sensing something was wrong between them, Veronica decided not to bring it up. Instead, she asked if they needed anything, and they both said no. Still, Veronica lingered for a moment, observing the two of them as she cleared the dishes.

Margaret was, as always, in control. Her words holding command, even though it was just the two of them, while Walt kept looking down, not participating. Veronica wondered what

Margaret was trying to get Walt to do, because that's what it felt like to her.

Returning to the chaos of the restaurant, Veronica's mind was spinning. Her instincts were telling her that something was wrong. Maybe because Emma's revelation earlier that day had set her on edge. And although Emma had shared something that seemed unrelated to the Mayor's death, Veronica couldn't shake the feeling that there was a connection.

However, Veronica felt hesitant about sharing her concerns. She was a mother and a waitress, not an investigator. Her world was her daughter and the steady rhythm of their life in Spring Falls, not the web of politics and secrets.

However, as she worked her tables, habit taking over, Veronica thought about how much Spring Falls and the friends they had made meant to her and to Emma, and she decided to keep her promise to Emma as soon as possible. They would talk to Judith and tell her what Emma had seen.

Yes, until now, she had preferred to stay out of things. Keep her distance. But their life had changed. She was part of something now. She was not used to sticking her neck out, speaking out about things, but as a mother, she'd do anything to keep Emma safe. And now they were part of Spring Falls, and she wanted to keep it safe, too. Besides, what Emma saw, and the haunted look in Walt's eyes, made her think that the two things went together.

Glancing back, she saw Margaret put money on the table and walk off without a backward glance. Walt stood for a moment looking so lost, Veronica stepped up beside him and asked if he needed anything else. And although he said he was okay, Veronica didn't believe it. He was so distracted that she had to remind him that his coat was on the back of the chair.

Once the crowd thinned out, Veronica went looking for Mary. She found her in the kitchen resting against a counter. Mary was one of the first people Veronica and Emma had come to know in Spring Falls, outside of the Ruby Sisters.

Mary was Bree's daughter, and Emma often babysat their daughter Rho, so they had grown closer as their daughters bonded. Emma said Rho was the perfect stand-in for a baby sister.

"Wow, what was that about?" Mary said, referring to the crowd they had just served.

"Bad weather, dead mayor?" Veronica laughed.

The two of them clinked their water glasses together and sighed. They knew the weather would change for the better, but what did a dead mayor mean for the town? That they didn't know.

# Twenty Two

Nancy watched as Judith helped Barbara and Tanner with their coats and walked them to the front door. Outside, the storm had gotten worse, and the two of them hesitated before stepping into it. She watched until she saw them get into Tanner's car before turning around to talk to Judith.

Knowing her boss as well as she did, Nancy could see that whatever had happened in Judith's office had upset her.

"Everything all right?"

"Not really. Since I have no more appointments today, I think I'll head home. And why don't you go home too? This storm is just going to get worse. It's probably better to leave now. I'll let Bruce know."

Nancy didn't need to be told twice. She was worried about the storm, too. But first she recorded a voicemail message saying the office was closed because of the storm, and then she was out the door and on her way home within five minutes. She had checked the weather earlier, and what had looked like a small snowstorm was turning into a Nor'easter.

And although the full force of those kinds of storms never came so far inland, they often caught the edge. And it looked like that was what was going to happen this time. She hoped it was the last one for the season. Like everyone else, she was ready for spring.

Judith waited until she was sure Nancy was safely out of the office and into her car before leaving herself. She refused to think about what Tanner and Barbara had told her until she got home. Otherwise, she was afraid she'd be too upset to drive safely. This was not the kind of weather to get distracted in.

Although the snowplows were clearing the roads as the snow fell, it was still rough going. When she pushed the remote on the garage door opener and saw Bruce's car already there, she sighed in relief.

Bruce also sighed in relief as he saw Judith's car drive into the garage. When Nancy called to let him know they were closing the office, he asked her to cancel his one appointment, too. Then he closed up his office and home and drove to Judith's. If he was going to be stuck in a storm, he wanted it to be with his wife.

It had been a busy morning. His first clients that day had been a young couple setting up their first will, as they were expecting their first child. On the other end of the spectrum, there were people coming to the ends of their lives, setting up new provisions for their loved ones. It was the part of his work that he loved.

And although sometimes he didn't want as much work that now came his way through referrals, he was grateful too. It was a mixed bag of feelings. He had planned to keep a small practice, but even though he didn't advertise, he was always busy. He knew he was going to need help soon, unless he stopped taking new clients. Maybe while they were stuck in the house together, he and Judith could talk it over.

But when he saw Judith's face as she came through the door, he knew that there was something much more pressing than his full calendar going on.

"I'll make coffee," he said, as Judith shed her coat and boots in the passageway between the garage and the kitchen.

Judith nodded and headed to her office to get her computer. There were a few things she needed to look up before telling Bruce what Tanner and Barbara had told her. Thankfully, she had the presence of mind to get their permission to get the help she needed.

At first, they had hesitated. When she reminded them that they had come this far and they needed to keep going, they agreed. Reluctantly. Judith knew how they felt. She was reluctant too, and she had done nothing wrong.

Or she hoped she had done nothing wrong. But years ago, when she worked for the Mayor, she had seen the papers that had put into place what Barbara and Tanner told her had been going on all this time. Young and inexperienced, she didn't know what they meant. But did that make her innocent in what had happened?

So she found herself caught between being frightened and angry. However, she knew that no matter what, even if she was partially unknowingly responsible for what had happened, she was going to fix it. And if she had to pay the price for their ignorance, or as in Barbara's case, looking away as a crime was being committed against the people of Spring Falls, so be it.

Judith knew Tanner and Barbara realized they were in trouble, although probably not Tanner. After all, he had known nothing until Walt hinted at it. It was Barbara who could suffer the consequences of what she hadn't done.

Judith had told them both that they would have to speak to Booker. But she'd do some research first. Maybe after the storm was over, they could make an appointment with him. They had both agreed. It had to be done eventually, and with Judith's insistence, they knew sooner was better.

Tanner said he was relieved, glad to not be the only one carrying the burden of knowing something was wrong, and not knowing how to fix it. Barbara had said she needed to make arrangements for her business, just in case things went badly for her.

When Judith came into the kitchen carrying her laptop, her face pale, Bruce put the coffee down, took the computer out of her hands, and hugged her.

"Before you show me what you obviously want to show me, why not just tell me what happened?"

Seeing the wisdom of his request, once again Judith saw why Bruce had become such a popular trust attorney. He listened with his whole being. When she finished, Bruce said, "I think we need to call Booker now and make an appointment for as soon as the storm is over."

Judith nodded in agreement. What neither one of them said out loud was that they were wondering how long this problem would have gone on if Marshall hadn't died. And Judith wondered if it was *why* he had died. Maybe it wasn't an accident after all.

# Twenty Three

"He was pushed," Booker said to Bree.

He had stopped at Bree's home on his way back to the station. He told himself that he wanted to make sure she was safe from the storm, but in truth, it was because he wanted to talk over with her what he had found out.

Bree's constant insistence on getting clarity about everything, from organizing her thoughts and her home, was both her gift and what she called her curse. Booker understood why she might think it was also a curse. She knew her constant need to know and make things clear sometimes drove people crazy. Including him. Especially if she kept interrupting as he was trying to explain something.

When he complained about it, she said she couldn't help it. She needed to hear everything to get it straight in her head. Perhaps it was what made her such an excellent writer. She couldn't let something go until she saw it clearly. She found the holes in everything that people said. "That doesn't make sense" was her favorite well-worn phrase.

And if you heard that, you had to be prepared to give her all the facts until it did. And if it didn't, well, then Bree said she knew what she had heard was a lie. Intentional or not.

Booker thought Bree should be the person all politicians had to get past before they could run for any political office. But that was another story altogether. Right now, he had to make sense of what he now realized. Marshall was pushed down the stairs on purpose.

So it was Bree's insistence that things make sense that made her the perfect person to talk to about it. Because even though it was clear to him that Marshall was pushed, he wasn't entirely sure why he knew that to be true, and he knew that talking about it with Bree would help him figure it out. This time, he wanted her to relentlessly ask questions until there was clarity about what had happened. Maybe then he could figure out why.

"He was pushed?" Bree asked. "How do you know that?"

The two of them were sitting at the kitchen table. Each of them had a cup of coffee and a plate of Bree's famous—to the Ruby Sisters, anyway—chocolate cookies within reach. Addie, his beloved rescue dog, was lying on his feet.

Addie stayed at Bree's most of the time now. Truthfully, so did he. He was rarely home because of work, but it was also because his two favorite beings in the world were right here in this house. For months now, Booker had been thinking that perhaps it was time to sell his home and move in with Bree. Bree had asked him to, and he kept putting it off. Not because he didn't want to, but because he was afraid. Why he was afraid, would have to wait for another time, because right now he had a murder to solve.

Bree asked her question again. "Seriously, Booker, how do you know he was pushed?"

Although shocked at what Booker had told her, Bree had done exactly what Booker hoped she would. She had immediately gone into the mode of needing to know everything so she could make sense of it. Because even though she accepted Booker might be right, why would someone murder Marshall?

She needed to rule out that it wasn't an accident. Or maybe he hadn't been pushed on purpose.

But as Booker answered her questions about how he knew, it was the missing computer that convinced her. Like her, Marshall was attached to his computer. It would never not be with him.

"Did you find backups? Thumb drives? Access to where he stored his stuff on the cloud?"

"Nothing so far. He had his home staged to sell. There was nothing personal left. So he must have had his backups with him. But we didn't find them. They weren't on him, or in his suitcase. Whoever took the computer, took those, too."

"Or he put them someplace safe here in town."

Booker shook his head. "It was obvious he was never coming back. He had a one-way ticket."

"So he was bugging out," Bree laughed. "I've always wanted to say that in real life."

Booker laughed with her. "Yes, he was bugging out. But why? What had he done that he was leaving behind?"

"And what could he have done that was bad enough to make someone kill him?" Bree added. "If we knew the why, we could narrow down the who."

Booker took a sip of his coffee, grabbed a cookie, and stood. "Thanks for letting me talk this out with you, but gotta go. Perhaps ask the Ruby Sisters to ask around if they have heard anything?"

"You mean like Judith?" Bree said, glancing at her ringing phone.

"He's right here. Do you want to talk to him?"

Hearing Judith's answer, she put the phone on speaker and set it on the table between the two of them.

"I'm here," Booker said.

"I need to bring two people in to see you that have something to tell you."

"Can't it wait? We're in the middle of a massive snowstorm, and I'm dealing with Marshall's death."

"That's the thing. The more I think about it, the more I'm convinced this has something to do with Marshall's death. Have you considered that it wasn't an accident?"

Bree and Booker looked at each other. Maybe this was the beginning of getting answers.

"I'll be right over."

"No, we'll both be right over. Can I bring Addie with me?" Bree said.

"The more the merrier," Judith laughed. She loved having people stay at her house. Although the word merrier was probably not appropriate given the circumstances. Nevertheless, she loved having company. No matter what the occasion.

# Twenty Four

Daniel and Cindy were in Cindy's art studio upstairs, deliberating on which pictures to display in her gallery in March. Out of the blue, Cindy blurted out the thoughts that had occupied her mind all day.

"I want to get back the picture I painted for Marshall. Do you think it's still in his house? What will happen to it if I don't get it?"

Daniel stopped what he was doing and turned to look at Cindy. Wearing sweats, with her hair messily pulled back into a ragged ponytail, and no makeup on, Daniel thought she was the most beautiful woman he had ever seen. But he had to laugh at the sight of her standing in the middle of the studio, hands on her hips, looking very determined.

"What are you laughing at?"

"You. So beautiful."

Cindy softened her stance a little and shook her head. She was no such thing. But if Daniel wanted to deceive himself that way, she would not stop him.

"I'm serious, Daniel. I want to get the painting back. Do you think I should call Booker and ask him when I can go get it?"

"Cindy, when people die, you don't get the paintings back you sold to them. Why would you get this one back? Booker can't just give it away. There are procedures. Maybe Marshall willed it to someone." And then, taking another look at Cindy's face, added, "Why do you want it back, anyway?"

Cindy sat down and looked up at the skylight, which was now covered with a few inches of snow, and thought about why she wanted it back so badly. Daniel was right. When a painting was sold, she let them go. They were no longer hers. What was it about Marshall's that made her want it back?

"Maybe I don't need to get it back. I just want to look at it. I did something different with this painting. Marshall asked me to paint something for him in the corner. He said it was important to him, so I did it. Now I want to see it again."

"Don't you take a picture of every painting? Don't you have one of Marshall's?"

Cindy snapped her fingers and pulled out her phone, scrolled through it until she found Marshall's picture. Enlarging it with her fingers, she got it as big as she could and then showed it to Daniel.

"What does this mean?"

What Daniel saw was a closed eye nested inside a triangle. A single vine wrapped tightly around one side of the triangle's border before reaching away.

"Do you know what it means?"

"He didn't tell me. And I think what's bothering me is that I allowed him to dictate what I put into the painting. Plus, there is something I don't like about the symbol itself."

As he stared at the symbol on Cindy's phone, Daniel had to agree. There was something he didn't like about it, either. He wondered what it meant. Closed eye, triangle, vine. Nothing strange about any of those things.

"Let's take each part of the symbol one at a time. Maybe we can figure it out that way."

Cindy said the closed eye seemed obvious. Not seeing. Daniel looked up the triangle and read that it was an ancient emblem for power and hierarchy. They both agreed the vine was growth.

It was Cindy who summed up what they had found. "Well, if we take this at face value, this symbol means not seeing the power and hierarchy growing out into the world."

"Well, that's freaking creepy," Daniel said. "Especially since Marshall liked it enough to ask you to put it into a painting. Was it a message about what he was doing or what he saw the world doing?"

"Well, let's hope it is not the former," Cindy sighed. "But have you ever seen this symbol anywhere else?"

Daniel shook his head no.

"Oh well, maybe it will come to us."

Cindy put her phone away, and the two of them went back to sorting through paintings. She decided it wasn't a big deal, but from now on she would not put anything in any painting that didn't belong there, no matter how important the client was.

And even if she couldn't get the painting back for good, she was going to paint out that symbol. It didn't belong. It creeped her out. Besides, Marshall would never know. And since it was so small, she was sure no one had even noticed, yet.

All she had to do was figure out how to get the painting back long enough to do it. Maybe she could ask Booker if she could hang it in her studio for a bit is a memorial to Marshall. And if not Booker, she'd ask whoever was in charge of Marshall's estate.

She wondered who that might be? Who was Marshall's estate attorney? To whom did he leave his belongings? Did he have any family? How did she not know anything about him other than that he had been the mayor of Spring Falls for so long that she couldn't remember when he wasn't.

After a few minutes of looking at paintings and realizing that she wasn't really paying attention to what she was doing, she decided to call Booker. Sure, he was busy. But what good was it to have a member of the Ruby Sisters dating the chief of police if you couldn't call him directly?

But it wasn't Booker who answered. It was Bree.

"Why are you answering Booker's phone?"

"He's in the bathroom and left it on the table. What's up?"

"I wanted to ask him about a painting I did for Marshall."

"Marshall. The topic of every conversation. Listen, we are heading over to Judith's to talk about something to do with Marshall. Why not come, too? Before the storm gets any worse."

"It's going to get worse?" Cindy asked, ignoring everything else Bree said. It already looked like it would be better to stay home. But then, going to Judith's sounded like an excellent idea. They had weathered many a storm at her house.

So, after saying they'd be there soon, she called Mimi at the gallery and told her the news about the storm. She told her to close up and get home before they got snowed in there.

Mimi said they were already making preparations to do so. No one was coming to an art gallery in this storm.

Satisfied that she had taken care of business, she and Daniel packed a few things just in case they got stuck at Judith's and headed over. Daniel didn't even bother to protest. Once the Ruby Sisters decided to get together, there was very little to stop that from happening.

Besides, even though he had never known Marshall, he wanted to know what was happening as much as anyone else.

# Twenty Five

Across town, Colin mulled over his missing cufflink. He pulled out the one that was still in his cuff and put it in his jewelry box. He had thought that he lost the other one when he and Marshall had scuffled at the party, but his contact at the cleaning company said no one had found it.

The scuffle was not one of his finest moments. He hated physical confrontations and avoided them at all costs. But Marshall had said he wanted to talk to him privately, and they had stepped into the storage room.

At first, Colin thought it was only going to be a private goodbye before Marshall went on vacation. Or maybe there was business he had to complete, and he didn't want anyone to hear.

Instead, Marshall was angry. He didn't like the way their last deal had gone. Colin had smirked at him, reminding Marshall that he was no longer mayor, and technically had no power to tell him what to do.

Marshall had not liked that answer and had grabbed his arm as Colin started to walk away.

"You'll be sorry," Marshall had said.

Colin had stared at him until he let go. And then to appease him—because after all, they had been friends and business partners for years—he said, "You'll be back and we'll deal with this problem then."

Of course, Colin hadn't known then that Marshall had no intention of returning to Spring Falls. Thinking about it now, Colin started to feel the familiar swell of anger rising in him, and he pushed it back down.

It didn't do any good to get angry. What was done was done. But it was hard to let it go. Marshall had been planning to leave them all with the problem of what they had done together. He deserved what he got.

As for the cufflink, it wasn't a big deal. Well, it was in a way because now he only had one, and with Marshall gone, he didn't know where to get another one. But Marshall being gone was a good thing, even though it didn't happen the way he thought it would. He'd keep the one cufflink to remind him once again to not trust anyone.

Outside, the snowstorm had taken a brief hiatus, and he wondered if he should try to talk to Margaret about Walt. If he headed to her house now, he'd be there before what was supposed to be the worst of the storm hit.

But then he might be stranded at her house. *On the other hand,* he thought, *that might not be a bad thing.* They had many things to discuss, and resurrecting their friends with benefits relationship might be the perfect thing to do in a snowstorm.

Colin picked up the lone cufflink again, rolling it between his fingers. Its cold, metallic feel reminded him of his relationship with Marshall. It was a custom piece, designed exclusively for their inner circle, a reminder that they were bound together by the decisions they had made together.

Staring out at the calm of the snowy landscape outside, he thought about what he had done. The lull in the storm was beautiful. It made the world seem so serene. A stark contrast to the tumult inside him. Things had changed drastically in such a short time, and despite his calm exterior about it all, he was worried.

Margaret becoming the leader of their group had always been the plan. And now, with Marshall out of the picture, she would move their previous plans forward sooner and without Marshall around to mess with them.

However, it seemed to Colin that those plans now had an uncertain future. Because Margaret was right, if they didn't strategize, the power vacuum left by Marshall's departure could be exploited by anyone.

With a determined nod to himself, Colin decided that confronting the storm was a small price to pay for securing his position in the town's political ecosystem. He bundled up, taking one last look at the cufflink before shutting the drawer of his jewelry box. It was like closing a chapter. Marshall was gone. He needed to move forward.

Driving through the flurries that had begun again, Colin's mind raced. If he and Margaret realigned, their combined resources and influence would be unparalleled. While Walt was a challenge, with Margaret's expertise in managing him, they might be able to put him to use. Barbara and Tanner were another story. What were they going to do about them?

The journey to Margaret's was slower than he'd anticipated, and the storm was picking up faster than he thought. But once Colin reached Margaret's driveway, he felt a sense of relief. Her home stood tall and commanding against the storm, a beacon of safety.

Parking his car, he took a moment to appreciate the surrounding serenity. The world was muffled under a blanket of white. His footsteps crunched in the thick layer of snow as he made his way to her entrance.

Margaret answered the door almost immediately. Had she been expecting him or someone else? Seeing Colin, her face showed a hint of surprise but quickly transformed into a knowing smirk. "Unexpected, but not unwelcome," she said, letting him inside.

The warmth of Margaret's house enveloped him, chasing away the chill. As they moved to the living room, with its roaring fireplace, he felt the gravity of their situation. This storm could be the perfect backdrop to forge a new alliance, one that would shape the future of Spring Falls.

They had plenty of time. No one knew what they had been up to, and no one was going to be running around in this snowstorm trying to figure out why Marshall had died. Besides, Colin thought, they wouldn't bother questioning it. After all, he had simply fallen down the stairs.

Which reminded him. He and Margaret needed to plan Marshall's funeral. How big of an affair could they make it? How could they use it to remind Spring Falls that Margaret was to be mayor and no one else?

Margaret poured them both a glass of wine and they settled on the couch together.

"We have a lot to plan," Margaret said.

Colin nodded. "That we do. But what about something pleasant to get us into the mood first?"

"Well, if you are referring to planning our future as leaders in Spring Falls, then yes. Let's do that. Very pleasant," Margaret said, moving a little away from Colin.

He smiled. She was right. Business was always a pleasant way to spend time together. And it was going to take some time to review everything. Looking outside at what was now a complete whiteout, he was glad he had decided to come to Margaret's.

He and Margaret were safe, warm, and prepared to do his favorite thing. Plan ways to make more money. And really, between the two of them, no one could stop them now.

# Twenty Six

"It's a snow day party," Cindy giggled when Judith opened the door. She and Daniel stamped the snow off their boots on the front porch and slipped them off as they came in the door. Two other pairs of boots sat on the rubber mat, and she let out a squeal of delight.

"Wait, are Bree and Booker here too?"

"We are," Bree said, coming around the corner to hug Cindy and Daniel. "And yes, it is a snow day party!"

"Are April and Marsha coming?"

Bree nodded no. "We called. They said they were just as happy holing up in the Ruby House. They were going to make use of the wood stove that they just had installed."

Cindy said okay, but in her heart she was disappointed. It would have been great to have another storm party. But perhaps April and Marsha were uncomfortable that Bruce, Daniel, and Booker were here. Now it was a couples snow day. Different.

"Want me to help in the kitchen?" Cindy asked Judith, who had come out of the kitchen to say hello.

"I'll entertain the men," Bree laughed. "Try to keep them out of trouble."

In the kitchen, Cindy and Judith decided to make dinner instead of serving snacks all day. They could order in pizza as they normally did when the group got together, but without April and Marsha it didn't feel the same.

Inspired by her visit to Doveland, Cindy made spaghetti sauce, while Judith prepared garlic bread and set the table. The two of them worked together without needing to talk. Friends since grade school, they knew each other well. It was in grade school that they had bonded along with Marsha, Bree, and April, and started calling themselves the Ruby Sisters.

But then Bree married Paul, moved away, and they lost complete contact with her. It was as if she had disappeared off the planet. April had left when she married Ron. And Marsha had moved to New York to pursue a career in dance and theatre. So for years, it had been just the two of them in Spring Falls.

Every Monday morning, they had coffee together, just as they had that morning. But other than Judith's weekly phone call with April and an occasional note from Marsha, for a long time they were the only Ruby Sisters left in Spring Falls.

And although Cindy had been happy running her art gallery, and Judith loved being the accountant everyone came to, they were both lonelier than they knew. And heartsick that they were no longer the Ruby Sisters.

But then Paul died, and all the Ruby Sisters received a letter he had written and given to his lawyer to mail after his death. He asked them to help Bree. They didn't hesitate. It didn't matter that it felt as if Bree had deserted them. She needed them now. It had been Cindy who had gone to get her, while Judith, Mimi, and Janet had kept the art gallery running in her absence.

After that, everything changed. Judith met Paul's attorney, Bruce. Bree found Mary, the daughter she had given up for adoption. Marsha fell in love with Nicky, the woman who brought with her the secret that April's husband Ron was a serial killer. And Robert, April's son, coming home to comfort his mother, brought his friend, Daniel.

And of course, by then every Ruby Sister had moved back to Spring Falls, so it was no longer just Judith and Cindy. Or even just the Ruby Sisters. Their family had expanded. Daniel found his half-sister, Veronica. Mary married Seth and had a daughter named Rho. Spring Falls had opened its arms to all of them and taken them in.

As Cindy stirred the sauce, she looked over at Judith and smiled. She didn't need to tell her what she was thinking. Judith nodded at the living room where they could hear Bree, Bruce, Booker and Daniel laughing, and smiled back. But Cindy was worried. Judith was unusually quiet. Was something wrong?

After dinner, they gathered in the living room around the fire. Judith had left the curtains open so they could watch the storm. It was completely dark outside, but the snow was so white it was hard to tell. Other than the wind howling in the trees, it was a white, silent world.

After a few minutes of gazing at the storm, Bruce spoke up.

"You've been extra quiet tonight, Booker. Anything you want to talk about?"

Booker looked at Bree, and she nodded. He repeated his concerns that he had told Bree earlier about Marshall's death ending with his belief that it wasn't an accident. Someone had pushed him and taken his computer.

Turning to Judith, he asked, "You said you had something to share about Marshall?"

Judith sighed. She should be happy about this mystery. It was something she could help solve, something she could fix. But this time, she wasn't sure that she could. And it was possible that she was partially responsible for what seemed to be happening. Not on purpose. But then how many horrible things happened because someone made a mistake? And this time it might have been her.

Still, it was not in her nature it give up or remain quiet about injustice, no matter who or what caused it or perpetuated it. Reaching over to hold Bruce's hand, feeling the steadfast strength he radiated, she answered.

"Yes. I need to tell you something I learned about Marshall and the Council. And if it's true, then the town of Spring Falls is in trouble. And even though I don't want it to be true, I think it is."

"It would explain Marshall's death?" Daniel asked.

"I think it would."

For the next hour, Judith shared with her best friends what Tanner and Barbara had told her. She couldn't prove it yet, but she thought it was true. The group took turns asking her questions, Booker watching more than talking.

And then the room fell silent. Outside, the snow had stopped falling, and the only noise was the distant sound of the snowplows as they began the work of clearing the roads.

It was Cindy who broke the silence by asking, "So there are many people who would have a reason to push Marshall down the stairs, aren't there?"

"Afraid so," Booker answered.

# Twenty Seven

The missing cufflink remained unnoticed in Pedro Santiago's pocket until Monday afternoon, when, as the storm intensified outside, his wife decided to do the laundry. Pedro returned home exhausted on Saturday after cleaning up from the Mayor's retirement party and forgot about the cufflink he had pocketed. Sunday morning had been filled with family and church, and then he was off to work at his other job. The one he liked, and would have liked more if he weren't so tired from working twelve hours a day at two jobs. Even then, they were barely making ends meet.

But working at ParaTi's as a line chef had reminded him of when, as a kid, he used to help his mother in the kitchen as she prepared food every day for their large family. He chopped, and cleaned, and peeled, and made food so good that sometimes people got tears in their eyes.

He wanted to be that person, be like his mother, make food so good that people cried for joy. Working at ParaTi's, he had felt a glimmer of hope that one day, he could be. But that glimmer grew fainter every day as he struggled to feed, clothe, and house his family.

Which was why the wasted food at the Mayor's retirement party was so upsetting. Why did people take food they weren't going to eat? He saw it all the time at ParaTi's. People ordering more than they needed.

But at least at ParaTi's, he and the staff could eat a meal, and any unserved food at the end of the night was available to anyone who wanted to take it home. Then, if there was still food, it went to an organization that distributed it to the needy. People like him.

On Monday, Pedro worked the lunch shift at ParaTi's. After lunch, because of the worsening weather, the management closed the restaurant, ensuring that the staff could get home safely. They had already begun preparations for the evening's dinners, which meant they had a lot of surplus food that wouldn't keep. Pedro took advantage of that and brought home enough food to cover lunch and dinner for him and his wife for a few days.

And since there was no cleaning work because of the storm, he was home when his wife, Maria, found the cufflink and asked, "Where did this come from?"

He explained he had found it while cleaning up after the party, and she asked why he had kept it. "Shouldn't you have turned it in to the boss?"

"Leon wasn't around. It was late. I stuck it in my pocket and forgot about it."

Maria turned the cufflink over in her hands, inspecting the intricate detailing. It was a handsome piece, with a crest she didn't recognize. She caught the faint glint of gold, indicating its worth was likely substantial.

"Look at this design, Pedro," she murmured, her fingers tracing the engraving. "It looks expensive, like something a rich person would wear."

Pedro sighed, thinking back to that night. "I think it belongs to one of the Council members. They were there, celebrating with the Mayor."

Maria's eyes widened slightly. "If it's from a Council member, then it must be very valuable. What if they are looking for it? You might get in trouble if they find out you took it."

Pedro shook his head. "I didn't 'take' it, Maria. I just forgot about it, that's all. I'll return it tomorrow., maybe there's a reward." he added hopefully.

Maria handed it back to him. "Just be careful. You know how these rich folks can be. They might accuse you of theft."

Pedro nodded, understanding her concerns. His boss, Leon Price, was not known for his depth of understanding and might accuse him of stealing it. The divide between the working class and the town's elite was clear, especially when it came to matters of trust. He carefully placed the cufflink in his pocket, intending to keep it safe until he could return it.

Monday night, Pedro couldn't sleep. His mind kept wandering to the cufflink, but more than that, to the inequalities in the town. How could some people wear such expensive jewelry while others, like him, worked tirelessly just to feed their families? The storm outside mirrored his inner turmoil, the wind howling, snow blanketing everything.

The next morning, Pedro decided. He would return the cufflink, but not to his boss. What good would that do? He would probably accuse him of stealing. Instead, he would talk to his friend Mary at ParaTi's and ask her to introduce him to the group of women that often came in to ParaTi's together.

He and Mary had struck up a friendship because, on her break, she would often watch him preparing the food. She told him she wanted to make better food for her husband and daughter Rho. Pedro had shared what his mother taught him, and Mary showed him pictures of her husband and daughter.

Mary had even introduced him to her mother, Bree, when she had come in with a group of women who called themselves the Ruby Sisters. In fact, she had introduced him to all of them, and although Pedro didn't think any of them would remember him, he would talk to them anyway. Especially the one with flaming red hair, because Mary had told him she was someone who righted wrongs.

And there was something very wrong going on in Spring Falls. It had been going on for some time, and no one had done anything about it. He hoped that Mary's mother and her friends didn't know about it, because if they had and had done nothing about it, then all was lost. He didn't know who else to go to.

If it was just him facing this problem, he probably wouldn't say anything. He had been taught to not make waves. But it wasn't just his family. It was an entire community of people who had been told they needed to move because their houses were being torn down.

Who gave them the right to demand that of them? Where were they supposed to go? Pedro knew it wasn't the first time this had happened, and he knew if he said nothing, it wouldn't be the last.

Yes, he would return the cufflink. But he'd ask Mary to help him take it to the red-haired woman named Judith, and that would give him an opening to explain what was happening to his neighborhood. He prayed she was not part of the problem, and that she would believe him, and most of all that she could—and would—do something about it.

# Twenty Eight

Colin had spent the night at Margaret's, but not in the way he had expected. Instead, she had given him a blanket and pillow and let him sleep on the couch in her office. And that was only because of the storm. Otherwise, he would have been shown the door.

In the morning, she had woken him up as soon as it was light, handed him a cup of coffee in a travel mug, and practically pushed him out the door.

It was an obvious message. Business only. At least Margaret hoped that was the message that he got. She had no more time for these side affairs. If Colin could do what she asked of him, they would be just fine. If not, then something else would have to be done.

When he had told her he had not yet approached the people she had asked him to about running for the Council, she had wanted to strangle him. Did he think he had the right to question what she asked him to do?

But instead, she had remained silent, waiting for him to stumble over himself with apologies. Which he did. And promised to take care of it immediately. She hoped he was telling the truth. Despite, or maybe because of, his arrogance, he was useful to her.

But now that he was gone, she had some serious thinking to do. Until Marshall's death, she hadn't realized how much of her power was because it was teamed with his. She wished she would have realized that sooner. She might have done things differently.

Instead, now she had to build up her power base herself. It pissed her off that it was so much harder for women, even women like her, who didn't back down. But she was up to the challenge. She always had been. This was nothing different.

On any other day, she would have left the house by now. She would first stop at the restaurant she owned for breakfast, and to check on things. It was just one of many businesses she owned in town, but it was the one she allowed people to know about.

Owning a small business that served people food came in handy. People loved to be fed. And she made sure she did that well. She often met people at her restaurant to discuss business. This way she didn't appear as if she was better than them. She was like them.

She had purchased the restaurant from the original owner as soon as she had some money, and then hired the best manager she could find. It was the place she and her friends would often go to after school, or after games, or dances. She liked it then, but she liked it better now that it was hers and she had made some changes based on what she had learned from her travels.

The changes were subtle, but they worked. That was her. Subtle. Not that people knew that. What they saw was the outward appearance that she projected on purpose. They thought she was one-dimensional, but she wasn't. And that, she decided, was where her true power lay. Behind the scenes. Let them see what they wanted to see. Diversion worked in magic tricks and in real life.

As she dressed for the day, Margaret thought about Marshall and what she knew about him that she assumed no one else knew. Should she go to Booker and tell him? Because eventually he'd find out, and then he'd figure out that she knew and wonder what else she was keeping from him.

As she applied her lipstick, Margaret thought she was aging well, but something felt off. In the mirror, her blond hair suddenly appeared too garish, and she decided that was the problem. It was too blond, as if she was still a young woman.

It was time to tone it down a little, maybe even let some gray show? It was trendy now to have pure gray hair, especially if it was more white than gray. She wondered what her hair color really was now. She'd have to find out.

It was a small decision, but it was the small things that people used to form opinions. She needed people to see her as wise and dependable. A little gray could help with that.

Still, she had to decide what to do about Marshall's secret. She almost wished he had never told her. But they had both drunk too much one night and were reminiscing about the indiscretions of their youth. Neither really ever shared anything that would give the other one power over them, so their conversations were rarely personal.

But then Marshall had paused and said, "I was married once."

She had laughed and said, "Yeah, right."

Turning to her, she swore she saw a hint of tears in his eyes, something she had never seen before, and he said, "Yes. I was."

"What happened?"

"I was who I am now, not a nice person, as you know. So within a year, she left me. I never even met him."

"Met who?"

"The boy. She was pregnant. She said she didn't want him to ever know me, just in case I influenced him in some way. When she sent me divorce papers, I barely glanced at them before I signed. She didn't ask for anything from me, so what did I care?"

"You didn't care that you had a son somewhere? How could you not?"

Marshall had shrunk into himself and didn't answer. Margaret was busy trying to figure out who that woman could have been.

Finally pouring himself another drink, he added, "Eventually, I decided I did care. I looked for them both. But by then, she had hidden herself and the boy completely. Now it's too late."

"Maybe you should look again. Technology is better."

"No. Too late to do anything about it. He'd be too old for me to mold him into what I wanted him to be. Which is exactly why his mother kept him away from me."

Margaret had nodded, and they both fell silent, ending the evening not long after that revelation. After that, they never spoke of it again. Marshall acted as if he hadn't told her, and she acted as if it didn't matter. And it hadn't. Until now. Because, if for some reason that boy, now man, showed up, he had a right to Marshall's estate. And that could cause all kinds of trouble.

So Margaret felt as if she was in between two hard decisions. Tell, and control the narrative. Not tell and hope that no one found out.

# Twenty Nine

By Tuesday morning, the roads were clear, and the snow had already begun to melt.

"February," Judith mumbled to herself as she opened the door of her office, trying not to slip on the slush that layered the sidewalk. Who liked it? Not her. Although there was already evidence of spring on its way, despite the snow, it couldn't come fast enough.

The holidays were fun with food, gatherings, and beautiful decorations. But she eagerly awaited the freshness of spring. She had often threatened to go away during the month of February. Wait it out in some place warm, like Hawaii. *Maybe next year,* she mumbled to herself.

Nancy, as always, was already in the office, had coffee brewing, and had a smile on her face. Judith had no idea how she would run her office without her, not that Nancy didn't remind her of that fact periodically.

"It's a full house today," she said cheerfully. Judith knew the cheerfulness was because Nancy loved being around people, and although she lived alone, often went out with friends after work.

Nancy had brought in many clients over the years just because she so often bragged about her boss.

By lunchtime, Judith was both exhausted and hungry. Since she didn't have a client for a few hours, she thought she'd treat herself and have lunch at ParaTi's. She texted Bruce to see if he could join her.

By the time she got to ParaTi's, he was already there, waiting at their favorite table, wearing one of the shirts she had given him because she thought it brought out his blue eyes. It did. To Judith, he was the most handsome man she had ever seen.

Judith thought back to when they first started seeing each other. They would meet out of town so no one would see them. She wasn't sure why they did that. After all, who would have cared?

Now it seemed as if half the restaurant smiled and waved as she made her way to the table. Bruce stood and gave her a quick hug before sitting again, and a little titter ran around the room as people smiled at one of their favorite couples.

As they settled in, both Mary and Veronica came up to their table.

"Wait, we get both our favorite waitresses today?"

"No, it's Veronica today, but we both have a favor to ask of you, Judith. I have a friend in the kitchen. Pedro. You've met him. He needs to talk to you about something he found at the Mayor's reception."

"And I have to show you some pictures of something Emma saw on her run this weekend," Veronica added. "Well, actually, Emma wants to show you, but I want to be there too."

"Are these two things related?" Judith asked.

The two women looked at each other before Mary answered, "On the surface, they don't seem to be, but we think they are. Somehow."

Judith held up a finger to ask them to wait as she called Nancy and asked her when she had a free hour that afternoon. Hanging up, she said, "Can Pedro and Emma, and of course you, too, Veronica, be there at 3:00?"

Veronica said they could and then stayed at the table to take their order while Mary checked with Pedro. As she hurried out of the kitchen to the table that was waiting for her to take their order, she gave them a thumbs up.

The atmosphere inside ParaTi's was warm and buzzing with chatter. This was Judith's escape from the mundane routines of life, a comforting space where familiar faces and mouthwatering aromas greeted her every time. But today, she had trouble enjoying it.

As she had listened to Mary and Veronica, she felt that now familiar undercurrent of worry grow. It was worse now, though. Because she now knew that underneath Spring Falls' peaceful surface, something evil had been going on for quite some time. And she thought that what Pedro and Emma had to tell her would add more proof.

Bruce had watched the exchange, intrigued, sipping his coffee. He and Judith had been through many adventures together, some light-hearted and others gravely serious. He always admired her ability to balance her dedication to her profession with her personal life with him and the Ruby Sisters.

And although she hadn't said anything, he knew she thought what Pedro and Emma had to tell her would confirm what they already had begun to uncover. It meant that they were on another adventure together. But a part of him was more worried than usual.

Despite both of them being worried, Bruce and Judith enjoyed their meal together. They laughed at shared jokes and discussed plans for the weekend. They decided that maybe they'd even go to the theater to see a movie. Something they hadn't done before.

But behind the casual conversation, Bruce could see Judith's mind working diligently, trying to connect the dots and prepare herself for the meeting with Emma and Pedro.

After lunch, Bruce walked Judith to her office, stuck his head in the door to say hello to Nancy, and then walked to his office to meet with his next client. It was someone who wanted to make sure his land went to the Green Zone Trust at his death. Bruce smiled to himself as he wrapped his coat around him and ducked his head at the chill wind.

The sidewalks had been shoveled, but they were still wet and a little slippery, so he was extra careful as he walked. The last thing he needed to do was fall and hurt himself, because as soon as the snow melted and it warmed up a few degrees, he planned to start running again. He had run in his youth, but had given it up a few years before meeting Judith, thinking he was too old to be running. But hearing about the runs that Daniel and Emma often took together inspired him to begin again. He didn't want to run far, maybe just to the Green Zone.

The Green Zone was one of the many reasons he loved Spring Falls. He knew that the circle it made around the town was almost complete.

There were just a few more tracts of land to add to it, and then the land around Spring Falls would be preserved forever as a place for nature to thrive. It would remain undeveloped except for the walking trails. He and Judith had explored some of the trails in the summer, and he couldn't wait to go back to enjoy them again.

Bruce was grateful that he could play a minor part in completing the Green Zone. But when his client arrived and Bruce saw the look on his face, something told him it would not be as easy as he thought.

# Thirty

By Tuesday afternoon, Margaret was exhausted. She shouldn't have let Colin come over at all. Should have turned him away at the door. Colin and his "I Know More Than You" intellectual attitude had always made her want to strangle him.

But he had once been useful, and sometimes fun. Not anymore. Once she was mayor, she would start cleaning out the Council. New blood. Hell, she could start now. She was acting as mayor. Now she was glad that yesterday Colin never got around to approaching the two people she had picked. She had been wrong. What she really needed were people who were beyond reproach. The goody two shoes of the world were going to be her new best friends. If the people of Spring Falls trusted the Council, they'd trust her as their mayor.

Which meant that she would not hide from Marshall's death and what could be revealed because of it. Instead, she'd get out in public and start talking. A press conference was a good start. This way, it would look as if she was in charge of finding out what happened. And when news started to leak out about the developments—which she was sure would happen at any time—she would be ahead of it and could control the narrative.

All she had to do was lie convincingly. Besides, even if someone realized she was lying, she'd just lie more. After all, she had sufficient evidence to prove that many people believed liars long after they knew they were lying, as long as the lies suited their agenda.

All she had to do was appear as if she was looking out for the common folks. She'd make them believe she cared about them and their tiny, insignificant lives. And when, and if, what she had done leaked out, she'd call all of them liars and accuse them of persecuting her for their own agenda. She'd model her actions after the person doing it now in her own country. It worked for him, it would work for her.

Margaret knew well that eventually what she and the Council had done would become public knowledge, and that's why there were only two possible courses of action: run or declare that she was innocent. It was a no-brainer of a choice. She wasn't running. She had spent her whole life preparing for this moment, and no one was going to take that away from her. The only solution was to claim innocence.

If Walter or Colin choose to run, that only made them look guilty, not her. She almost wished they would. Having them around could complicate things.

But even though she would claim that she was innocent and knew she could pull it off, she wasn't stupid. Since the moment Marshall had died, she had begun destroying anything that might point to her. She had been shredding and burning documents for days. She was burning them because Margaret knew that there were machines that could put shredded documents back together. And even though there couldn't possibly be one in Spring Falls, she wasn't taking any chances.

Right now, her living room fireplace was full of shredded documents going up in smoke. That was one good thing about the snowstorm and the cold. No one would wonder why there was smoke coming out of her chimney. She had logs in the fireplace with the paper so that the smoke looked like wood smoke. If she had to stay up all night to make sure every trace of what she had done was gone, she would. She had destroyed the online documentation first. All of this was because she was sure Booker would soon come calling.

As for Walt and Colin, she wasn't really worried. They had no official documents, and if they kept their own records and tried to release them, she'd accuse them of fake news. That included all the other people they had bribed to look the other way, or to change zoning requirements. No one actually ever saw her. It was always Marshall. And since he was now dead and his records were gone, he couldn't accuse her of anything.

Margaret knew it meant all the developments they had been doing and were planning were over. Margaret was sure Booker would soon find out enough to have all construction stopped. But it was over anyway the minute Marshall died. Actually, she had seen the end of everything months before when Tanner started asking questions. She thought she could control him, but it didn't take long to realize she had made a mistake with him.

Stretching her long legs out as she sat at her desk, she sighed. She hated shutting everything down. What a loss of money it was going to be! But perhaps once this was all over, she could begin again, legally this time. In the meantime, she had enough money put away where no one could find it that would last her a lifetime if she wasn't too extravagant.

And even if they found the corporation and the money that Marshall had taken, it didn't affect her. And Marshall had stored it safely away where no one in any country could touch it. Eventually, she might find a way to get to it, but she was going to let it go for now.

What was important was that she was Acting Mayor now, and would soon be the Mayor. All of this was just a stepping stone. So whatever it took to get elected, she would do it, and that meant first getting rid of all the evidence that she had any part in Marshall's scheme.

Part of her wanted to apologize to Marshall. She had been his friend and partner for years. But she stopped herself from feeling any guilt. After all, he was the one who had betrayed her. He had been planning to leave town and never come back. Leaving them all with the mess he made—setting all of them up to take the hit for what he had started.

Well, he had underestimated her. Everyone always had.

# Thirty One

By 2:45, Veronica, Pedro, and Emma were at Judith's office, having decided to all go there together. Pedro was grateful that Veronica and Emma included him. This whole thing made him nervous. Would Judith believe he found the cufflink and didn't steal it?

A cluster of comfortable chairs made up the waiting room in front of Nancy's desk, and the three of them sat there, not saying anything. Emma got her phone ready to show Judith the pictures. With nothing else to occupy her time, she shuffled quickly through her Instagram, stopping to look at dancers, birds, and videos, barely noticing anything else.

At exactly 3:00, Nancy, efficient as ever, ushered them into Judith's office, made sure they had what they wanted to drink, and closed the door behind her, wishing she could have kept the door open. She wanted to hear what was happening. She knew something was up, something different. Nancy couldn't wait to have Judith fill her in on what it was about.

To Nancy, it felt that ever since they had found out that Marshall had died, everything was out of place. His death was like a massive windstorm sweeping through life in Spring Falls, reordering some things, toppling others, while revealing something rotten inside, like an old tree.

In Judith's office, Pedro was having trouble sharing. Everyone waited patiently until Judith said, "It's okay, Pedro," and he believed that it just might be. Sighing, he reached into his pocket, and with a trembling hand gave the cufflink to Judith.

"I didn't steal it. I found it."

"Well, of course you didn't steal it," Judith said, smiling at him, feeling the heft of the cufflink in his hand, thinking he was worried over nothing. But then, seeing how serious he was, she paused. She didn't live his life. A life where some people assumed people like him were thieves.

"I'm sorry, Pedro, that you would need to worry about such a thing. Tell me where you found it. And it feels like you have more you would like to tell me. Don't be afraid. I'm listening."

Looking at Veronica and Emma for encouragement, Pedro told Judith where he had found the cufflink and had simply slipped it into his pocket, forgetting about it and taking it home by mistake. He explained he was worried that if he returned it now, his boss wouldn't believe him and would accuse him of stealing.

And then, taking a deep breath, he also told her that he and his neighbors were being told they had to find someplace else to live, but none of them had enough money to move. And even if they did, where would they go? Each day brought them all closer to being evicted, and they were terrified.

As he talked, Judith felt anger override the worry she had been carrying around. Controlled anger was something she treasured. It meant there was something she could do. Worry never seemed to bring a solution to anything.

"This is wrong, Pedro. I promise to find out what is going on, and if at all possible, put a stop to it."

"These pictures might have something to do with it," Emma said, holding out her phone.

"This is in the Green Zone?" Judith asked, her voice tight.

"I think so. It's why I brought it to you. Perhaps I'm wrong. But what if I'm not?"

For Judith, things began to click together. What Barbara and Tanner had told her, Pedro being forced to move, and now construction where there shouldn't be. Finally, she was seeing how all of it connected. Now, she had to prove a crime had been committed and stop it from continuing.

And she was sure this was why Marshall had died. Someone thought they could cover it up. But they couldn't. Because she was going to do something about it.

Pedro stared at Judith. He had heard that when she got angry, her red hair flared and thought it was a myth. But now he saw it was true, and he was extremely glad that it wasn't him that her anger was directed at.

He almost felt sorry for who she was angry with. Almost.

# Thirty Two

Judith walked Emma, Veronica, and Pedro to the door, assuring them she would take what they told her and do something about it.

"I am sure I'll still need your help, but don't worry, we'll stop what's happening."

As she buttoned her coat, Emma told Judith that once the snow cleared, she was planning to go back to the Green Zone and take more pictures. Both Veronica and Judith wanted to tell her not to, but knowing that she'd do it anyway, made her promise to be careful. When Emma said she'd ask her uncle Daniel to go with her, they were both relieved.

Pedro shook her hand and said, "Thank you for helping us."

"I have done nothing yet," Judith answered.

"But you will, I know," he said, smiling, adding to himself, *I hope it's in time.*

Judith walked back to her office, closed the door, and placed a phone call to Booker. When he answered, she said, "I have more information to share with you about what we think Marshall and the town council have been doing. Did Tanner and Barbara come to see you?"

There was a long silence. Judith looked at her phone to make sure the call was still there.

"Booker?"

"Yes." Booker answered so quietly that she could barely hear him. "Yes, Tanner is here. But Barbara is dead. Tanner found her."

Tanner sat in the police station holding his head in his hands, bent over, his elbows on his knees, trying to keep himself as still as possible. *Breathe in, breathe out,* he was saying to himself. It was a trick his mother taught him.

Inside, he sobbed the word, "Mom." When he was in school and bad things happened, she was always the first one there to comfort him.

"It's okay," she would say to him, holding him tightly when he was young, and patting him on the back as he got too old to be hugged. Or so he told her then. But now, he'd do anything to have her be there, enfolding him in her arms.

And that it was impossible for his mother to ever comfort him again made him want to cry. Out loud. Not care that he was in a police station.

When he felt a hand patting his back saying, "It's okay," for a minute, he almost believed that he was wrong. His mother hadn't died years before. She was there now. For him.

But then he recognized the voice and knew it was Judith. Tanner still wanted to turn and sob into her arms, but he stopped himself. He barely knew her. He was a grown man.

Still, she kept her hand on his back until he was able to sit up and look at her.

When she said, "I'm sorry, Tanner," he believed she was. But why did people say that? They did nothing wrong. What were they sorry for?

Still, he had been trained to be polite, so he said, "Thanks." And once again, his brain asked him why he said thanks to something so stupid. Thanks for being sorry? No, he was thankful that she was there.

So he said, "Thanks," again, adding, "For being here."

News of Barbara's death spread like wildfire through Spring Falls, just as it had the day before over Marshall's death. With whispers now suggesting Marshall's death was no accident, rumors ran rampant. Had Barbara met a similar fate? The town, once shaken by Marshall's incident, now trembled with anxiety and unease.

In Judith's office, the phone rang non-stop. Nancy patiently responded to each call, reiterating that Judith was out, and they had no more information than anyone else. She tried to reassure the callers, promising that Judith would get to the bottom of it and all would be well.

But internally, doubt gnawed at Nancy. She suspected Judith might be holding back some details. And, given the sudden shift from a harmonious town to one clouded in fear, Nancy felt the residents' dread might not be misplaced. The conversations between Judith, Tanner, and Barbara worried her. Had they missed a crucial opportunity to intervene?

She imagined Judith grappling with guilt and questioning if they could've done something more to protect Barbara and Tanner. The snowstorm had falsely lulled them into thinking they had time. They were blindsided by the harsh reality that time was, in fact, running out.

Yet each time the phone rang, Nancy's professional demeanor didn't waver. She comforted and reassured, emphasizing Judith's commitment to the townspeople. With every repetition of "Yes, all is well," she felt a small flicker of hope. By day's end, she almost believed her own words. Almost.

# Thirty Three

argaret heard the news from Colin, who had heard it from a friend in the police station. He thought she'd want to know right away. She did.

When he called, she was still sitting at her desk in her home office, having never made it out of her house. There had been too much shredding, burning and deleting to do. She thanked Colin for the call, hung up, and then allowed herself a minute to feel sorry for Barbara. But she had no time to think about sorrow. Everything was falling apart.

She needed to make a plan for the Council that would work. Now she needed to replace three people. The only bright spot was that she had already decided to recruit people who questioned nothing and were not greedy. Compliant and not greedy. How many people did she know like that? Not many. But she'd find them, and that was that.

In her heart, Margaret knew she was doing the right thing by closing down what they had been doing with Marshall. She didn't want to, but she had to. She was on her own now. There was no one she could trust.

Within minutes of Colin's call, her phone rang again. She ignored it. It rang again. She ignored it again. But then, glancing at the number, she recognized it as the manager of her restaurant. Annoyed because he had other people he was supposed to call, and never call her directly unless it was an emergency, she answered with a harsh, "What?"

After a long pause, when Margaret had almost hung up on him, he finally said, "Heard through the gossip going around the restaurant that Barbara is dead."

In her head, Margaret said all the swear words she could think of, but to her manager, she quietly said, "Thanks for letting me know," and hung up. Furious. How did that news get all over town so quickly?

Things had gone from bad to worse, and once again, it occurred to Margaret that with Marshall dead, she had no one at all to trust or help her. She was on her own, and she wasn't all that sure she knew exactly what to do now.

After his call to Margaret, Colin texted Walt, "Did you do it yet?" All he got back was an angry face emoji. What was he supposed to do with that? Yesterday, he had called Walt before going to Margaret's house, and had expected that Walt would get a move on and get it done. Did he? There was no way to know.

Colin was in a foul mood. He had been that way since coming back from Margaret's house. Staying overnight on her couch was not the way he liked being treated.

He had come home, showered, making sure every trace of Margaret and her house, which now smelled like smoke as she burned papers, had been erased. He agreed with what she was doing about the papers and the files, but the whole thing had been humiliating.

Not that Margaret knew how he felt. He would not show her any kind of weakness. So what if she didn't want to play around anymore? He didn't care. He wasn't attached to people like that, even Margaret. But he hated being humiliated.

Marshall had loved finding little ways to humiliate him in public. It had been subtle, but it was always there. Marshall was always telling him what to do, expecting he would jump and get it done and then making cutting remarks about how it was done. He made it sound like praise, but it wasn't, and everyone knew it.

Margaret and Marshall were both like that, thinking they were the ones in charge. They were always subtly finding ways to belittle him. Well, now Marshall was gone, and Colin knew Margaret was panicking. Even though that involved him, he found a bit of pleasure in it.

But that pleasure was overridden by concern about his part in the situation. And even though he could tell he was sweating and his hands were shaking more than usual, he would not panic. He would keep his cool and take care of what he could before he would do what Marshall had been planning to do. Leave town. Forever.

He was done with Spring Falls, and soon Spring Falls would be done with him. If it was the olden days, they would ride up on their horses with a noose in their hands. Now it would be police sirens and a jail cell. He couldn't live with that.

But before he could leave, he had a few loose ends to tie up. Although Margaret was doing a great job of shredding and burning documents, there were other things to do. And Walt was supposed to be handling them. All he could hope for was that the angry emoji from Walt meant he was taking care of it, and he couldn't be bothered at the moment.

In the meantime, he would do what Margaret and Walt expected of him. Margaret had turned the planning of Marshall's funeral over to him. And that meant phone calls, and meetings, and more paperwork.

But if he planned it correctly, all eyes would be on the ceremony, and no one would look his way while he cleaned up his messes and prepared to leave town. Would he stay long at the funeral? Not if he could help it.

But everything changed again for Colin when he got the call from his friend at the police station and heard that Barbara had died. More complications. And with Walt not answering, he was at a loss. Things needed to be cleaned up and that he couldn't do. Who could if Walt didn't?

Then Colin thought of Leon Price. Leon had keys to almost every business in town because his cleaning company had contracts with them. Maybe he would ask him. Leon was involved enough that he might be willing, maybe even anxious, to do what needed to be done.

On the other hand, maybe he wouldn't wait. He really didn't care what happened to anyone else involved in their schemes. They could handle things themselves. Perhaps he should leave now. But first, he wanted Walt to call him back and let him know if he'd taken care of what he asked him to do.

And then Colin had a thought. All eyes were on Marshall's death and now Barbara's. Who would look his way? They'd be too busy handling the mess that their dying would make.

Maybe the best thing to do was to make a run for it now. Screw Walt and Margaret. Especially Margaret. He'd always had an escape plan ready. Why not put it into action now?

# Thirty Four

The Ruby Sisters had a direct line to Judith, bypassing Nancy entirely. Yet, even to them, Judith remained guarded in what she revealed when each of them called. However, instead of ending with all is well, she asked each of them to meet at her house that night.

When she talked to Cindy, she asked her to get everyone there.

"Everyone?"

"Yes, everyone. We are going to need everyone's creative thinking. But tell them all to keep quiet about it."

She didn't really need to say those last few words. Cindy would know.

At the last minute, she added, "And ask Nancy, Mimi, Janet, Emma, and Veronica too."

"You really mean everyone, don't you?" Cindy laughed. "I'll get a few more pizzas."

"What are you doing?" Tanner asked after overhearing Judith's conversations. She had remained with him at the police station and was sitting beside him as she fielded one call after another.

Judith looked at him and made a quick decision. He was the one who told her what he thought was going on. He was the one who brought Barbara in. She was going to trust him. So she told him to come to the meeting at her house.

"Don't speak to anyone about what happened or about the meeting, Tanner. Except Booker."

"I don't know what happened. That's the thing. After we told you what we knew, I was worried about Barbara. She was so upset with herself. I told her it would be okay, that we would be part of the solution. Barbara wasn't even worried about going to jail. She said she deserved it. She should have stopped what Marshall was doing when she first heard about it.

"So I thought I would go see her, let her talk it out, and maybe she would feel better. Besides, I thought she knew more than she told me and you. Maybe she would tell me the rest if she trusted me more.

"But she didn't answer the door, and it wasn't locked, so I stuck my head in and called for her. Then I saw her on her couch. I thought she was asleep, but something didn't seem right, so I went into the living room to check.

"I touched her arm, and when she didn't move, I called 911. Booker came right after that and brought me back here."

Booker, who had been listening to their conversation, added, "Emergency dispatch informed me about Barbara. The mayor and a Council member dead within days? Plus, after what you told me, Judith, I was more than a little worried."

"You'll be there tonight, too?" Judith asked.

Booker nodded. He didn't need to add that he needed all the help he could get. His small-town police force was ill-equipped to handle two suspicious deaths. Even if Barbara had died naturally, it didn't change that the Town Council—and who knew who else—had been up to something illegal that affected the entire town.

Which meant, in some ways, everyone in town was a suspect if they had found out what the Council had been doing. He had to narrow down the possibilities and figure out what was happening before another death occurred. And he needed help.

Judith asking the Ruby Sisters to help was definitely not protocol. But he knew they were his best chance of getting this handled as quickly as possible. Hopefully, before the entire world heard of it, and reporters descended on the town.

They had only discovered Marshall yesterday morning. And it was still only a suspicion that someone had pushed Marshall down the stairs. He could deny that it was murder for a while longer.

Yes, he would assure the town; it was a tragedy that two prominent members of the community had died in such a short time. But he would remind them all not to jump to conclusions. However, Booker knew it was a losing battle. The town had already jumped to conclusions. But it might buy him a little time.

Booker decided that the first thing he needed to do was appoint Judith as a deputy. That way, she could hear every detail of what he knew without causing a problem. Plus, the town trusted Judith. They knew she wouldn't rest until they solved the mystery and everything had returned to normal. Whatever that would look like now.

If he had to, he'd appoint every Ruby Sister as a deputy. They needed to figure out what was happening before someone else died. And knowing them, they were his best chance of getting answers.

# Thirty Five

Judith's living room was so full of people that it was hard to see who was there, and she wondered if she should have held this meeting somewhere else. But this was the most private place she could find. At least for a meeting planned at the last minute, as this one was.

For future events, she'd need to find another place because it looked like their once-small group was going to continue to expand. Her neighbors would know that something was happening at her house, although they wouldn't know what. However, knowing Judith, they might suspect it had to do with Marshall and Barbara's deaths.

Right before hanging up with Cindy, Judith decided to have her ask Mary and her husband, Seth, to also come to the meeting. Seth and April worked together renovating properties in town, and since Seth was a contractor, Judith thought he might know more about what was going on. Maybe he had seen something and didn't realize what it meant.

Now Rho was upstairs, sleeping in one of the spare rooms. Bree or Emma were usually their babysitters, and since they couldn't find anyone else at the last minute, they brought Rho along with them. No one minded. Rho was loved by everyone there.

It amazed Judith that Rho had fallen asleep given the noise level happening downstairs. Everyone was talking and laughing, despite suspecting what the meeting was about. They were using it as an excuse to catch up with each other and have some fun before things got serious.

Booker was not participating. He stood on the outside of the crowd, wanting to get on with it, continually glancing at his phone to keep up with what was happening at the station. Judith felt as anxious as he did, so once the empty boxes of pizza were stacked in the kitchen and all the paper plates had been cleared away, they nodded at each other, and Judith stood.

It took a moment for everyone to settle down. Watching all her friends talk and giggle together, Judith decided that this summer she would throw a party for these same people in her backyard. But first, they had to clear up this mess and get life back to normal. But like Booker, Judith understood that normal would not be what they knew before. She just hoped they could fix what had happened before more people died and before Pedro and his friends and family became homeless.

Standing with her back to the hallway, Judith waited until everyone turned their full attention to her. It didn't take long. Judith's hair had flared for a minute, and they all knew what that meant. Something serious was going on, and Judith wanted to fix it. Booker stood quietly beside her, ready to answer questions if needed.

After thanking them for coming, Judith raised her voice a little so everyone could hear.

"It all comes back to what the Council has been doing. Someone either didn't want it to come out or wanted to punish them for what they were doing."

Marsha raised her hand.

"I'm not clear about what they were doing. And who are they? Marshall and Barbara?"

Marsha realized that she and April had missed out on something by not coming over during the storm yesterday afternoon.

"Right, sorry. More details. Yes. Marshall and Barbara and the entire Town Council have been up to something that no one seemed to know about. Or at least no one spoke up about until recently. What we have found out so far is extremely basic, with very few details. And we only know this much because Tanner and Barbara brought me their concerns yesterday before the storm shut everything down. Barbara said she knew more, but she had to think about what she could tell me.

"'I need to gather my courage,' is what Barbara told Tanner and me. And of course now she is dead, so she can't tell anyone. The question is, did she die because someone knew she was going to tell more? But we don't know yet if it was a natural death or not. Booker is waiting for the answer."

"And then Emma brought pictures," Veronica said.

"And Pedro told you what was happening to his community," Mary added.

"Oh my God," April said. "Seriously. What are you talking about? Start at the beginning."

Everyone nodded in agreement.

For the next thirty minutes, Judith did her best to explain. She explained they had learned that Marshall and other members of the Town Council had been buying up land around town and forcing people to move using the claim of Eminent Domain. They told the people that their land had been bought by the town, which it hadn't. Instead, it was Marshall and his collaborators who were putting in new developments.

"How did they manage to do that?" Marsha asked.

"Barbara said they paid off many people to look the other way. They then transferred the land to a corporation comprised of

Marshal, Margaret, Colin, and Walt. Barbara explained she knew about it, but didn't take part. But she didn't report it either."

Tanner broke in to tell them that Walt had hinted at this to him when he took over as his accountant after his previous one died.

"I think Walt wanted to get out of this, which is why he told me."

"Or he wanted you to join in, or at least look the other way the same as Barbara did," Judith said.

Tanner nodded in acknowledgment, and Judith continued.

"And then there's the Green Zone. As you all know, a Trust protects it. Nobody can build there. And yet, it appears that someone is putting in at least one development, and we assume that this is also part of Marshall's plan."

Bree raised her hand. "So you are saying that members of the Town Council have been developing parts of the town illegally, including in the Green Zone? How did no one notice before? That seems impossible."

"Perhaps they were counting on people being too distracted with other things. And then, of course, there were payoffs made."

"Well, someone must have noticed," Marsha said. "After all, someone pushed Marshall down the stairs. Either they were angry enough to kill him or after something."

A murmur of agreement went around the room.

"How many people are affected?" Cindy asked.

"We don't know. We only became aware of this yesterday."

April and Seth looked at each other. How had they not noticed? After all, they were renovating buildings in town. If anyone should have noticed, it should have been them.

"What can we do?" Emma asked. "Can you stop them from making Pedro's family have to move?"

"That we can do," Booker answered. "I can have a judge freeze all building developments in Spring Falls with a preliminary injunction until we find out who is doing the developments and if they are legal or not.

"In this weather, there is not much development they can do, anyway. But once the injunction is filed, the remaining members of the Council, and anyone else involved, will know we found out what they were doing, so we'll have to move quickly."

Upstairs, Rho started to cry, and when Seth and Mary got up to take her home, Judith declared the meeting over. Everyone had a job to do, even if it was as simple as paying attention to what they saw and heard in town.

After everyone was gone, Bruce put his arms around Judith and she leaned back into him. He knew what she was thinking. This was her town. She'd find out who killed Marshall and stop whoever was involved in the illegal developments.

But Judith wasn't kidding herself. She understood that it was entirely possible that she'd uncover things she didn't want to know. But she'd do it anyway, even if it broke her heart.

# Thirty Six

By Wednesday morning, the storm that had dumped almost two feet of snow had vanished. In its wake, it left cloudless blue skies along with tree limbs bent over from the weight of the wet snow. Streets and sidewalks were a gray, slushy mess.

Every once in a while there would be the sound of snow falling from the branches, making a squishy, plopping sound, which was better than hearing the loud crack as a branch would fall off the tree. *Either way, walking in the woods is a bad idea,* Emma decided as she sat in the coffee shop.

But she was going to do it anyway. She wanted to take a closer look at the developments that she had seen. Yes, Booker and her mom—well, everyone — had told her to stay away. But she had decided not to listen. And she decided not to take Daniel. She knew he and Cindy were busy preparing a show. After all, how many people would be in the woods on a day like today?

And she was prepared. Instead of running shoes, she was wearing hiking boots. And because it was still cold, she had on her favorite pink puffy jacket with a hooded sweatshirt underneath.

Her jacket was currently hanging on the back of a chair at the coffee shop so everyone could see her sweatshirt that said, "I Dance."

Emma loved that sweatshirt. It had been a gift from Marsha, who had given every student in her dance studio one for Christmas. And even though Emma thought of herself as a painter, she definitely danced, too.

She realized she loved to dance after getting over her anger towards everyone, especially her mom, for making her do something she didn't want to do.

And now, once she fully realized that dance was art in motion, she was grateful that she could express art in that way, too. In fact, Emma agreed with the saying on the back of her sweatshirt that life is a dance, or art in motion. That meant everything she did could be considered art. Art wasn't just a painting on canvas, it was the way you lived life.

She had just read Thoreau's quote, "To affect the quality of the day, that is the highest of arts. Every man is tasked to make his life, even in its details, worthy of the contemplation of his most elevated and critical hour." Emma had decided to make what he said her life mission.

She would affect the quality of the day in everything she did, and right now, that meant she would not sit back and let bad things happen. The development in the woods was like slashing through a masterpiece. Not a canvas, but nature.

Sitting in the corner of the coffee shop, sipping her coffee and picking at her bagel, Emma watched the people as they came in, ordered, and then either left or settled into a table, sometimes alone, and sometimes with others. She wondered what each of them would do if, and when, they discovered that people they trusted were making money by destroying people's lives.

Would they explain it away to themselves? Say it had nothing to do with them? Or would they decide to learn more, and then do something to fix the problem? She thought most people would look away. They'd say they had work, or family, and not enough time.

Would she become one of those people who only noticed what affected them? Would she start to believe lies people told because it was easier? Would she listen to people as they said, "Don't make waves?"

Could she remain an artist of life, an artist in life, and fight for beauty and the rights of others? She hoped so.

When the door opened and her Uncle Daniel and Cindy walked in, Emma took it as a sign that she was on the right track. She loved and admired them both and knew they would choose to do the right thing. She waved them over to the table and when they nodded yes, she pulled another chair over. It would be a cozy fit, but she knew they wouldn't mind.

"I love that you're here," Cindy said, as she unzipped her coat and slipped it onto the back of her chair. "We can share our news with you. We could have shared it yesterday with everyone, but it didn't seem the right time."

Turning to Daniel, she said, "You tell her."

Emma's eyes started to fill with tears, as she looked at two of her favorite people in the entire world, who looked so happy she could have painted a brilliant white aura around them and it would have fit in.

"You can tell, can't you?" he asked her.

"When?"

"As soon as possible. I've waited long enough."

"But not until this mess is settled," Cindy said, reaching over and holding Daniel's hand and locking her hazel eyes onto his blue ones.

"You haven't told the rest of the Ruby Sisters? You told me first?"

Now the tears that had threatened started to fall. For the longest time, it had just been her and her mom. Moving from place to place. Now, since moving to Spring Falls, they had found family and friends and people that loved and supported each other.

It was a magical place and once again she vowed to herself that she would let no one destroy it. She would not sit back and say nothing when people lied and did terrible things to each other and nature.

But Emma said none of those things to the two happy people in front of her. She only smiled through her tears and told them how happy she was. "And did you realize that you'll be my aunt then?"

Cindy nodded, tears in her own eyes. "I did. Why do you think I said yes?"

They all laughed then, Daniel only pausing for a minute wondering if that was true, and then laughing again. He didn't care at all why Cindy had said yes. It was that she did, and he didn't doubt for a second that she loved him the way he loved her. He couldn't blame her for not falling for a ten-year-old boy she only glimpsed in the doorway of his father's art studio.

But from that moment on he had decided to be a man that someone like that goddess wearing paint spatter clothes, blond hair piled on top of her head, would consider worthy to spend time with.

That they had found each other was a miracle. That she had said yes was another. And although they had kept their voices quiet, their joy at their table seemed to spread out across the room as everyone turned to smile at them.

Emma looked around the room and, knowing how fast news traveled in Spring Falls, said, "You two better go tell all the Ruby Sisters now."

Cindy looked around and understood what Emma meant. It was time to go share some good news with her best friends before they learned it from someone else.

Hugging Emma goodbye, they rushed out the door carrying their coffees and laughing.

Watching them go, Emma sighed. They wouldn't be happy if they knew where she was going, but she was doing it for them, and for every person who lived in Spring Falls. And afterward, she was going to Pedro's to see where he lived, and find out how she could help him too.

Her mom had given her the day off. She was going to make the most of it.

# Thirty Seven

J oy and determination might have been what was going on at the coffee shop, but it was a different story at Tanner's house. He had rolled over in bed, groaned, feeling like a hundred-year-old man. He had the fleeting thought that he was too young to be feeling this terrible. But then he remembered all that had happened in the past two days, and his aches and pains seemed minor compared to the worry and anxiety that had invaded his being since he had heard about Marshall's death.

Tanner pulled the covers up over his head, blocking out the sun that was peeking through the crack in the curtains. Usually he was so careful to make sure there was no way to look in or out, but today it amazed him he had even remembered to close them. He had barely made it to bed the night before. He had come home from the meeting at Judith's exhausted, disgusted, and so sad he could barely think straight.

Although on one hand he was grateful that he had been invited to Judith's—after all, he had approached her—on the other, it had just increased the burden he felt he had been carrying around for weeks. He had wanted to speak with Judith to lighten that burden. Instead, it had just gotten worse.

Which wasn't Judith's fault. But whose fault was it? No one knew. Just that two people he had known and become part of his world had died. Nothing was good about that. It didn't matter that perhaps they had been doing all the terrible things that Judith suggested. And based on the evidence they had now, most likely it was true.

It was simply the fact that he had known them. Talked with them. Laughed with them, and in Barbara's case, had comforted her. It was that they died. He hated death. It was so final. He did not know what happened to people when they died. He hated it because it was the people who were left behind who suffered. Like him.

There was only one time in his life that he had felt worse than this. It was the day his mother died, something he tried not to think about. But now, with all that had happened, all those feelings had come rushing back. So here he was, a grown man, hiding under the covers, curled up in bed, wishing he was a little boy again, and his mother was with him.

As a child, when he was upset, she would come in and rub his back and tell him that everything was okay. She'd tell him that even when they both knew that things were not okay. She'd say it, he'd let himself believe it, and in that moment it was true.

All he ever wanted was for things to be okay. Some people might yearn for more than that. But for Tanner, okay would have been enough. But even as a boy, he knew that thinking something didn't mean it was true, or could make it come true.

Nothing would stop the kids who made fun of the geeky skinny boy, who had no sports ability and found it hard to talk to people who were being so cruel on a daily basis. For them, he was the sport.

Even now, he was the geeky man. Still skinny. Still not able to play a single sport. That the world had changed and made being geeky kind of cool, seemed only fair, but it didn't change how hard it was for him to fit in.

Not that he didn't try. He did. He worked at it. Studied what clothes he should wear to fit in. He learned how to speak well so he could explain himself better. Discovered that asking other people questions and then listening as they answered made him liked by most people he met. No one seemed to notice how ill at ease he was most of the time.

Numbers made sense to him. People did not. When he was a boy going to school, every day was a mixture of the pure pleasure of learning and the torture of not fitting in and being accepted.

But then, his mom was always there, doing her best to help him, even though there was not much she could do. "Life can be unfair," she'd say, adding, "but then it can be glorious too. Try to focus on the good." And for her, he did, and sometimes that worked, and he'd feel better for a while, at least.

As long as he could remember, it had been just the two of them. He hadn't minded that much. In many ways, just having his mother had been enough for him. She was the kindest person he had ever met. She worked hard, sometimes doing multiple jobs to make sure she could pay the rent, buy food, and keep the boy who kept growing out of his clothes dressed well.

And because he loved her, he never told her that the other reason they teased him was that he only had a few shirts and pants. One pair of shoes. To the boys and many girls in school, he was a fatherless poor boy, too tall, too skinny, glasses, too quiet, and too clumsy.

To make matters worse, he and his mother had moved a lot. Sometimes he was glad that they did, even though it meant starting over again. There was always the chance that at the next town, the next school, he would fit in. Eventually, he managed to look like they did, but he was always the new boy, so he never had time to make friends before they moved again.

After his mother died, he had moved to Spring Falls. It wasn't that far from where he had been living, and he thought he remembered his mom mentioning it once. It was as good a place as any. He wanted a place where no one knew him. Where he could start a new life, begin his practice as an accountant, and finally, maybe make friends. And he had. And now two of them were dead.

Lying in bed watching the sun dance over the patterns in the quilt his mom had made him years before, he thought about what she would say to him right now. "What about friends who haven't died?" she might ask. "How can you help them?"

And that made him think of Walt. Where was he? He hadn't seen or heard from him since the Council meeting on Monday afternoon. Was he okay? Walt was both a client and a friend, and he hadn't talked with him yet.

*How selfish is that?* Tanner thought to himself. *Walt had to be struggling, too.* Maybe Margaret and Colin were also having a hard time, but Tanner wasn't worried about them. The two of them knew how to work the system. But Tanner knew Walt was trying to be someone better than he had been.

Throwing the covers off, Tanner sat up in bed, only mildly surprised to see he hadn't taken off his socks the night before. Heading to the shower, he made a list in his head of things he needed to do.

Call Walt. No, go see Walt and make sure he's okay. Call Margaret and ask if I can help with Marshall's funeral. Check in with Booker to find out if there is any more news about how Barbara died. He knew Barbara's son's family lived out of town, but they would come in to handle her funeral.

Ticking items off in his head made Tanner feel better. And then he'd check in with Judith to find out how he could help with uncovering what the Council had been up to. After all, he was a member of the Council. He should be able to find out what they were doing. And it was Walt who might know the most.

*Yes, Walt first*, Tanner said to himself, pulling on his heavy winter coat, already feeling better. But first, a stop at the coffee shop for fortifications.

# Thirty Eight

Cindy and Daniel laughed together as they walked the few blocks to her art gallery. They took their time, saying hello to people as they passed and gazing into shop windows. Cindy thought they were probably doing that so they could see themselves in the window. She loved the way they looked together.

When they reached the gallery, instead of going in the back way, they burst through the front door, ready to share their good news. Cindy glimpsed one of her paintings hanging on the wall, and that intensified her joy. All the years she had been afraid to let people see her art, and now it was finally hanging on her own gallery wall, the way she had always dreamed that it would.

For years, she had suffered for no reason. Then Daniel had come into her life, and she had learned the truth. Daniel's father, Cedric, her revered art teacher, had lied to her when he told her she wasn't an artist. Then Cedric copied her art for years, becoming famous while she hid what she was doing in her house, not letting anyone see because she thought it wasn't good enough.

Now it was all out in the open. The lies had been exposed. The ones Daniel's father had lived and told her. The ones she had been telling herself.

Hearing the door open and Cindy laughing, Janet turned around from where she was arranging flowers in the corner, and stared at the couple. But only for a moment. Then, jumping up and squealing, she ran to them, hugging them both at the same time. Not an easy feat, given that she was so much smaller than the two of them.

Cindy often thought of Janet as the elf of the art gallery. Tiny, with spiked blond hair, today tipped with blue. Janet was wearing high-top sneakers and a bright pink sweater that swirled around her as she stepped away from them, bouncing on her toes.

Mimi, her partner in the gallery, and Janet's wife had stepped out of the back office to see what was going on—the picture of quiet elegance. Mimi, with her long dark hair lying sleek down her back, dressed in slacks, a jacket, and stacked tie-up shoes, looked as if she belonged in a fashion magazine.

"Congratulations," Mimi said, hugging them each.

"But how do you know?" Cindy said. "We only just told Emma."

"At the coffee shop," Daniel said, realizing what had happened. They had dawdled on the way. Someone had gotten there first.

"Yep, at least one person stopped by to say how happy you were when they saw you there and what they overheard."

"That's Spring Falls," Cindy laughed, and then stopped. "Oh my God, what if the Ruby Sisters find out before we tell them?"

Mimi laughed. "They are on their way."

Even as she spoke, they saw Judith almost running down the street. If the sidewalks weren't so slushy, Cindy was sure she would be running. Then they heard the back door open, and April and Marsha spilled into the gallery.

Judith reached the front door as Bree stepped out of her car carrying a box of donuts. Within minutes, Daniel and Cindy were surrounded by Ruby Sisters, and then dragged into the writer's room, everyone laughing and talking about how happy they were.

Mimi brought in a pot of coffee, and after everyone's cups were filled, they toasted the happy couple.

Daniel, the lone man, felt as if he had invaded Barbie Land. But he didn't mind. In fact, he loved it. This was all because he had asked Cindy to marry him, and they were happy about it. How could he complain about that?

The Ruby Sisters had embraced him the minute he had arrived in Spring Falls, a friend of April's son, Robert. Struggling with his father's death, he felt as if Robert had rescued him and then brought him to a place where the girl he had fallen in love with at ten happened to be living and where friends dropped everything to celebrate together.

Did he believe in miracles? Yes, he did.

The celebration didn't last long. Everyone ate at least one donut, toasted the couple again with their coffee, and wheedled out of the happy couple as many details as possible. And then they headed home after extracting a promise to have a proper party after the mystery of the two deaths had been solved.

No one added that they would wait until the corruption in Spring Falls was eliminated. They still didn't know exactly what had happened, or how long it would take to unravel it.

"Before you go," Cindy said to Judith, "Could I ask you something?"

"Anything."

"It's probably not that important, but I did a painting for Marshall, and I would like it back. Or at least back long enough to fix something in it."

Seeing Judith's puzzled face, she added, "There's a symbol he asked me to add to the painting, and I don't like that I did that. For one thing, I don't normally do that kind of thing for clients, but he was so persuasive, I did it against my better judgment. And for another, I don't like the meaning of the symbol. Or at least what Daniel and I think the symbol means."

Judith made a motion for Cindy to continue. She'd been doing that same motion since they were kids, so Cindy just smiled at her and continued.

"It's a closed eye inside a triangle with a vine wrapped around one side before reaching away. We think it means not seeing the power and hierarchy growing out into the world.

"It was as if he was stating his mission. Not that we knew it at the time, but hearing about what the Council has been doing, I think he wanted to have power with no one knowing it.

"I don't want that on any painting of mine, you know what I mean? Can you help me get the painting?"

"I'll talk to Booker, but in the meantime, I have something to show you. Tell me if it's the same symbol."

Judith reached into her pocket and pulled out the cufflink that Pedro had given her the day before.

Cindy gasped. "Where did you get this?"

"Pedro found it on the floor after the party when they were cleaning the room. He asked me to give it to Booker, and I forgot to because of Barbara's death."

Holding the heavy gold and black cufflink in her hand, Cindy nodded. "Yes, it's the same. And now I think I've seen this before. I never got close enough to see what was on it. I think this is Colin's. He's the only person I know who wears cuff links."

"Well, if it is his, then we have a provable connection between Colin and Marshall doing business together."

"Or it was just a gift," Daniel said, having stood listening to the two of them.

"True," Judith said, and Cindy nodded. But none of them believed that. And Judith was determined to prove it.

# Thirty Nine

Emma was getting ready to leave the coffee shop as Tanner arrived. As he opened the door, he immediately spotted her distinctive pink jacket. While he had seen her at Judith's meeting, they had never actually spoken. Tanner had wanted to introduce himself, but the crowd, combined with his distress over Barbara's death, had kept him quiet, limiting his interactions to brief greetings to those sitting nearby.

He had barely even spoken to Emma's mother, even though he wanted to. He knew Veronica from ParaTi's, and when he admitted it to himself—which wasn't often—he knew he was besotted with her. A strange word that, but it felt like the perfect one to describe how he felt about her.

The first time he had seen Veronica was when the Council had met at ParaTi's. He had fallen in love with the restaurant and tried not to think that he might also have fallen in love with the tall woman who moved like a dancer and smiled at everyone.

He couldn't acknowledge such a thing to anyone. He could barely admit it to himself. However, he started eating at ParaTi's as much as he could without raising suspicions, and he always tried to sit at one of Veronica's tables. Tanner wasn't sure if she had noticed him doing that, but over the past few months, she would often pause and chat for a minute.

Recently, during a quiet mid-afternoon visit to ParaTi's after a client meeting, Tanner found the restaurant empty. Taking advantage of the open time, Veronica joined him at his table. She introduced him to her world by sharing a photo of her daughter, Emma, and spoke passionately about Emma's love for art. Veronica also recounted their journey, describing their many moves before settling in Spring Falls.

She shared how happy she was when she discovered she had a half-brother, Daniel, who arrived in town with Robert when he visited his mom, April. Both of them had agreed that there must be some kind of force that moves people towards each other. And if they were open to it, they would notice and accept it.

Veronica confided in Tanner that Emma had always been the center of her world, because there were just the two of them. But when they moved to Spring Falls, they had both made friends and met so many people they liked that they decided to stop moving and stay. And now they were both much happier.

Tanner didn't think he would find a missing family member in Spring Falls the way that Veronica had, but at least he was making friends. Trying not to think about how he had lost two of them in just the last few days, he made a decision. He stepped out of line and headed off toward Emma before she went out the door.

"Hi, I'm Tanner Foster. I know your mother, and she showed me your picture. And of course, I saw you at the meeting yesterday."

Tanner wanted to sink into the floor. He thought that was the stupidest introduction ever. But then Emma smiled at him, and he felt better.

Emma looked at the tall thin man standing awkwardly in front of her, and realized he felt embarrassed, and she understood what it took for him to come over to say hello. She often had the same problem.

Besides, her mother had told her about a dark-haired man who always sat at her tables and then pointed him out at the meeting. She was happy to finally officially meet the man her mother talked about, unaware that she often blushed as she did so.

Smiling at him, she said, "Hi. I saw you at Judith's too, but my mom had already told me about you."

Tanner took a step back and could feel his face turning red. Could it be true she talked about him?

"She did?"

"She did. Said you were a nice man and fun to talk to. I'd stay and talk, but I have something I need to do."

Tanner nodded and stepped away, too afraid to say anything else in case he blurted out things that he shouldn't say. Like, I think your mother is the most beautiful and kind woman I have ever met.

No, he couldn't say that. So instead, he stood transfixed as Emma left the shop. When she turned to wave as she went out the door, he managed a wave in return.

Stepping back into the end of the line, Tanner thought about what Emma had said. Veronica had talked about him? Was it weird that it made him happy to think that she did?

Taking a seat, Tanner opened his computer to get some work done. Maybe being around people would help him think better. For the next few hours, the murmur of people coming and going helped him concentrate.

Sometimes he saw people he knew, and they'd stop by the table and chat. Often he'd hear people discussing Marshall and Barbara and wondering what was going on in Spring Falls, but he refused to be drawn in.

Working at the coffee shop was going so well, Tanner got a sandwich and soda and settled back in again. Hours later, he was caught up. Except for his work with Walt. He needed more information from him.

So, ordering a coffee to go, Tanner packed up and texted Walt to tell him he was heading his way. And even though he didn't get a reply, he decided to go anyway. Maybe Walt was trying to avoid thinking about what had happened, and had buried himself in his work.

Walt's bookstore was only a few blocks away, nearer to the campus. Walt always carried books students needed to read in class. However, ebooks had taken over much of his business, and Tanner knew Walt had been struggling to figure out ways to keep his business afloat.

That worry, plus the two deaths, was a good reason for Walt to stop answering his texts. At least, that's what Tanner told himself. He refused to worry that another one of his friends might be in trouble.

But when he got to the bookstore, and it was closed, his heart stopped beating for a moment. There was no way Walt had intentionally closed his bookstore. Peering through the front window, he saw Walt's bright blue glasses lying on the floor.

Walt wore bright framed glasses hoping that people would think about going to the bookstore that the guy with the glasses owned. He had told Tanner he liked the idea of it because it helped people remember him. Otherwise, why would they remember a guy who was average in every way? An old man with gray hair and a bald spot.

Tanner dropped his coffee cup, not even noticing that coffee sloshed onto his shoes, and reached into his pocket for his phone to call Judith. He needed her to help him. He couldn't bring himself to call the police station. What if Walt had simply knocked his glasses off the counter and hadn't noticed?

However, while his phone rang, Tanner kept saying to himself, *No, no, no, not another one.*

# Forty

Emma laughed to herself as she headed towards the woods. She wondered if her mother knew that the man she described as nice and fun to talk to was in love with her. What would she think? Would her mother like that? Respond in kind?

And what would that mean to her? Would it be okay if her mother started dating? All those thoughts ran through her head as she tramped off to the Green Zone. She wished she were running. She'd be there so much faster. But the snow meant no running, just trudging, so it took her almost an hour to reach where she had been on Monday when only a little snow had covered the woods.

Now it was a wet, sloppy mess. With each step, her boots sank below the surface, snow coming up past them, some of it slipping wetly down behind her socks. She knew that meant she would probably have blisters when she took her boots off.

What had she been thinking? She could have waited at least one more day before coming here. The sun was out. The snow was melting. By tomorrow, it would almost be gone. And the development would still be there.

But that was hindsight. She had made it this far. She was going to check it out. Then she'd have something to report. She'd walk through it, take some pictures, and share them with Judith.

As she got closer to the development, Emma thought she saw someone move between the buildings. But when she looked again, not seeing anyone, decided it was just her imagination working overtime.

Huffing from exertion, from having to lift her feet so high for each step, she made it to what appeared to be a road. *A street,* she wanted to yell. Right in the middle of the Green Zone. And a lane had been packed down in the middle of the road, making it easy to walk down. *Or drive down*, Emma thought.

*Don't get mad now*, Emma, she said to herself. *Take pictures and get out. Get mad later. Maybe walk out following the road, see where it goes. It will be easier than tramping through the snow.*

Looking back at where she had come from, she could see her footprints, the edges of them melting. It would be even worse going home. Yes, she'd try the road and see where it took her.

Once again, she thought she glimpsed something moving between the buildings, but could see nothing there. She could tramp over to the houses and see if there were footprints. But she didn't, admitting to herself she was afraid to look.

*Take the pictures and get out*, she said again to herself. Holding her phone up, she started snapping pictures of the partly finished buildings beside the road and then switched to video as she walked down the road. All she wanted to do now was get out of the woods and back to town.

But she still had to prove what she was seeing. Otherwise, who would believe what was happening here? She had to have evidence so someone could make it stop.

• • • ● ●• ● ● • •

Marsha had an idea. She wasn't sure it was a good idea, or that it would work. But it kept niggling at her, and finally she had decided that if it didn't work, it would be just one class and no one would be that upset.

Besides, she was the teacher. And if she wanted to shake things up a bit, she could. And she was definitely ready to shake things up. Like many people, she disliked February in Pennsylvania. Although there were signs of spring in February, like the birds building nests, those signs were hard to find amidst the mostly gray days filled with either slush or mud.

Her idea was to teach a hybrid ballet class once a month, maybe more if the students liked it. She'd start with a five-minute warm-up using Sun Salutations and warrior poses. Then a shortened ballet bar, finishing on the floor doing a few Martha Graham movements.

Next, instead of going straight into the ballet phrases, they'd do ten minutes of something like hip-hop. For Marsha, this sounded like a fantastic way to introduce her dancers to multiple forms of movement, which was so necessary in today's dance world. But perhaps it would also inspire them to find expanded and creative ways to do anything. Also necessary in the real world that was constantly changing.

Her dance teacher had often said she wasn't building great dancers, she was growing good people. It had taken Marsha many years to understand what she had meant. If some of her dancers went on to make it their profession, that was lovely, but what she really wanted was to make a tangible difference in the quality of life her students experienced. One thing Marsha had vowed to herself was that she'd turn none of the classes they held at The Ruby House into competitions. Dance was an art, and she'd keep it that way.

Standing in the dance studio, a cup of coffee in her hand, Marsha watched the sun shine through the branches of the maple tree in the yard, causing large piles of snow to slide off and plop into the yard. She had to admit that it was beautiful. Maybe she should expand her thinking and learn to like February.

Besides, with no leaves on the tree, she could see into town. It was interesting to watch people, many of whom she knew, walking, going in and out of shops, and talking together. Earlier that morning, she had seen Emma heading towards the woods, and realized that if no one else liked the hybrid class, Emma would. She'd do it for her and see what happened.

# Forty One

Margaret watched the last of the paper burn in the fireplace as she buttoned her coat. She couldn't hide in the house for one more minute. It was making her stir-crazy. Besides, people expected leadership, and she was going to give it to them.

Earlier, she had made a series of phone calls and set up appointments with everyone from the funeral director to an event planner—a funeral was an event, or at least it would be this time—and a press conference.

It wasn't much of a press conference. They only had a small weekly newspaper in town and an online version that people mostly used to check on what was happening in town and who had died. But it was the idea of it. Margaret needed to tell Spring Falls that all was well.

The police would handle what happened to Marshall, but she would handle what happened after Marshall. It was up to her to turn his death into a new beginning. And if what he had been doing came to light, she would lie her way out of it and come out of it shining as a beacon of hope for Spring Falls.

That Barbara had also died was sad, but Barbara had never been a power broker in town. She'd offer to help plan a smaller funeral for her. Maybe find out who inherited her nursery. Maybe buy it from them and turn it into something special.

The more Margaret thought about the future, the more energized she became. On her way out the door, she texted both Walt and Colin to meet her at the town hall. "Now!" she emphasized.

By the time she started her car and was pulling out of the driveway, already cleared of snow by her handy man who always did her house first if he knew what was good for him, Colin had answered. Hearing nothing from Walt, she thought about driving by his bookstore and finding him, and then decided not to.

She'd send someone to find him later, and give him a talking-to. Disappearing on her was not a good idea. For a moment, she thought of getting Tanner to also come to the meeting and decided against it.

Yes, he was a member of the Town Council, but not for long. He had turned against her when he went to Judith. He'd find out what that meant for his future in Spring Falls later. But first she had to build up her image and remind people she was now the acting mayor, and would soon be the mayor. It was time to act like one.

Veronica checked her phone and saw that Emma had left the coffee shop and was walking towards the woods. Shaking her head, she sighed. If she had known that was what Emma was planning, she would have told her not to go.

On the other hand, would she have listened? Telling Emma not to do something she was determined to do would be like telling the wind not to blow. Over the years, Veronica had learned that the best she could do was to keep watch over her daughter and remind her to think before acting.

Putting her phone away, Veronica headed to work. She had given Emma the day off from homeschooling, not just so she could have a well day off from school, but also so that she could have some time to herself. After work, she planned to go home, grab a book, and snuggle up in her favorite chair and read.

All that was going on in Spring Falls was so stressful Veronica wanted to not think about it if only for the afternoon. But when she got to work, Pedro was there waiting. And when he asked her if she had heard anything, Veronica realized her daughter was the one who was right. Emma was trying to do something about the injustices that were going on.

Pedro didn't have time to curl up in a chair and read a book. His family was in trouble. What Veronica needed to do was to help him. There would be plenty of time to read books after she helped stop the Council, or whomever was responsible, from taking his and his friends' homes.

Thinking about Emma trudging through the snow to get answers, because she was sure that was why she was doing it, Veronica decided to be more like her daughter. After work, she'd go to Judith and ask her what she could do. Maybe she could do research that Judith didn't have time to do.

But for the next few hours, Veronica didn't have a chance to do or think about anything other than taking orders and clearing tables. She expected it. After every snowstorm, it seemed more people would come to lunch. Maybe just grateful to be up and about and safe from the storm.

Or maybe because during storms the power would often go out in different parts of town, so heading to places that still had power or had a generator running was a wise thing to do. For whatever reason, Veronica was busy. She didn't mind. On days like this, people seemed to tip better.

It wasn't until much later that she thought to look at her phone to check and see where Emma was. She expected her to be home by now, probably wet and cold. She would see if Emma wanted some food from ParaTi's and treat her to whatever she wanted.

But when she looked at her find-a-friend app, it didn't register where Emma was. It was annoying, but she wasn't worried. That happened from time to time. It worried her a little that it probably meant Emma was still out in the woods, but she was sure that Emma would pop up soon. She had a dance class later that day, and Veronica was sure Emma wouldn't want to miss it.

# Forty Two

Booker found Tanner walking back and forth in front of Walt's bookstore. When he saw Booker, Tanner stumbled towards him, saying, "Please, please, don't let him be dead."

"He's probably at home, Tanner," Booker said, holding Tanner still by the shoulders. "This is not the time to fall apart."

He had sent one of his deputies over to Walt's house to check, but had come to the bookstore himself, because of Tanner. He understood why Tanner was so frantic. It was Tanner who had found Barbara.

All that had happened in the last few days was not Tanner's normal, orderly life. Not that it was his life, either. Spring Falls was known for its low crime rate and friendly citizens. But as he said to Tanner, it was not time to fall apart, and that meant him too.

"But I'll check here too if you really think there's a problem. We'll go in the back way so we don't break down his front door."

"I have a key."

Booker stared at Tanner.

"He gave it to me. I'm taking over as his accountant, and he wanted me to be able to come in at night when he has the door locked if I needed anything."

"Then why didn't you just go in?"

Tanner dropped his head, and Booker put his arm around him, understanding why.

"Okay, we'll go in together."

Taking a deep breath and willing himself to keep his eyes open, Tanner opened the door and held it open so Booker could go in first. He had no desire ever again to find someone the way he found Barbara. It would haunt his dreams forever.

And as Booker walked through the bookstore, Tanner stayed by the door in case he needed to run. Tanner tried not to think that probably made him a coward. Besides, his fear had him rooted to the spot as if someone had glued him to the floor.

A few minutes later, Booker returned, holding Walt's glasses in his hands, having picked them up off the floor.

"He's not here. And I just learned he's not at his home either. Do you have any idea where he is?"

Tanner shook his head. He didn't know Walt that well. Pointing at the glasses that Booker had put on the counter by the cash register, he asked, "Why would his glasses be on the floor?"

"Perhaps he brushed them off on the way out. I think he has many pairs. He might not have missed them."

"I guess," Tanner answered, "But it feels like something is wrong."

Booker didn't disagree. Something didn't feel right to him, either. It was time to talk to Margaret again. She feigned distress the last time and told him nothing. This time, he'd take Judith with him. It was hard to resist Judith's questioning.

"Do you want me to take you home, or do you want to come with me to talk to Margaret?"

Booker thought that taking Tanner too might trigger a reaction in Margaret. Between the three of them, they might get more out of Margaret than if he went alone.

Waiting for Tanner to answer, Booker called Judith, who said she'd be right there. As Tanner looked around the bookstore, he thought of Walt, Barbara, and Marshall. He needed to do something. If Margaret knew anything at all, she needed to tell them before anything else happened.

Besides, if his mother had been there, she'd tell him it was his duty to help. Just thinking about his mother and how much she had taught him about life, Tanner relaxed. He was not a coward. He was not timid.

He would be what his mother had told him to be. Strong and kind. She believed that those two qualities made good people, and that's what she expected of him. Now was the time to prove it.

"Coming with you," he answered.

By mid-afternoon, Veronica was no longer a little worried. She was terrified. She had moved past being angry with Emma for not being home when she got there. Now, not being able to see her on the find-a-friend app, and not being able to reach her on the phone, Veronica felt helpless.

Trying to calm herself down, she reasoned that perhaps Emma went straight to dance class, and didn't realize her phone was off. Maybe she had her dance stuff with her and she hadn't noticed.

However, when she called Marsha and learned that Emma hadn't shown up for dance class, Veronica went into full-blown panic.

"What do I do?" Veronica practically yelled at Marsha.

"I saw her walking towards the woods this morning. Do you think she might still be there?"

But then, not waiting for an answer, Marsha said, "Stay there. I'm going to get help and we'll go look for her."

"No. I have to come too."

Realizing she couldn't stop her, Marsha confirmed Veronica would be there in a few minutes, and then called Daniel. She briefly explained what was happening and that they needed to search the woods.

When he said he'd be there in a few minutes, Marsha relaxed a little. Daniel would know what to do.

Marsha thought of calling every Ruby Sister and asking for help, but thought first they should check the woods. There was no point in scaring everyone. Daniel and Emma often went running together, and Marsha thought he might know how to find her.

April came out of her office to find out what was going on and disagreed with Marsha.

"We need everyone. It's going to be dark in a few hours and very cold. You, Daniel, and Veronica go to the woods. But I am calling everyone else to have them check in town."

"Including Booker?" Marsha asked.

"Yes," April answered. She didn't need to add that the last few days had turned the idea of Spring Falls as a peaceful, safe place upside down.

It was totally unlike Emma to simply disappear. There was something wrong, and pretending like there wasn't would not help.

# Forty Three

Booker, Judith, and Tanner sat opposite Margaret and Colin, each with a cup of coffee before them.

Tanner had tasked Judith to guide the discussion. He hoped Judith's friendly approach would encourage Margaret and Colin to be more forthcoming. While suspicions surrounded the duo regarding Marshall's death, they didn't possess concrete evidence that they had anything to do with it. Besides, they weren't prepared to broach the sensitive topic of the town's dubious redevelopment plans just yet. They needed proof first.

Instead, Judith gently steered the conversation towards Marshall's upcoming funeral and the future of the Town Council. Margaret, acting as the spokesperson for the pair, detailed their plans. Throughout Margaret's explanation, Judith responded with affirming nods while taking notes. Colin remained silent, but appeared to support everything Margaret said.

For the time being, they all appeared united in their aims. However, when Judith inquired about Walt's whereabouts, Margaret's face clouded with worry as she answered.

"We've both tried to get ahold of him since yesterday. Do you think there is anything wrong?"

As Tanner observed the dynamic between Judith and Margaret, he likened them to two sides of the same coin. Strikingly alike, yet poles apart. They both scared him. But Judith's presence was a challenging yet positive force, urging individuals to rise to their best selves, and sometimes that was a scary thing to do.

Margaret scared him in the same way spiders scared him. She had a knack for luring people into her intricate webs, manipulating them for her own gain. She'd done it with him, drawing him into the murky dealings of the Town Council. Only now did he truly understand that everyone around her was mere prey.

Though it wasn't something he could yet prove, the realization was so profound that he almost blurted it out. But observing Judith's tactful interaction with the pair, he held back.

He didn't want to give away what he thought. Margaret believed he was a pushover. He'd let her go on thinking that, while he found proof of what was happening. Walt had hinted at it and given him the keys to his store and his house. He must have wanted him to find something.

Was Walt always planning to leave, and let Tanner discover what Margaret and her friends were doing? The answer yes was so obvious, he gasped out loud.

When everyone turned to look at him, he said, "Sorry, I just realized I need to be somewhere right now. Sorry everyone, I have to go."

Just then, both Booker's and then Judith's phones rang. They excused themselves, stepped away, and listened. Watching both of their faces change to worry, Tanner felt his fear rise again. Something else had gone wrong.

Booker turned to Margaret and Colin. "We have to go too. But if you hear from Walt, let me know."

He slid his card across the table to the two of them. Of course, they knew his number, but this was serious business, and he wanted them to have no doubts that he wanted more information from them.

Once the three of them were outside, Booker told Tanner what the calls were about. Veronica's daughter, Emma, was missing.

"I just saw her this morning,' Tanner said. "She was heading for the woods. But that was a long time ago. I need to help."

"Didn't you have something else to do?" Judith asked.

"Yes. But this is more important."

Judith, who noticed everything, had seen Tanner stare at Veronica as if she were a goddess. And since Veronica didn't seem to mind, she told him to go to the Ruby House where he'd find Veronica.

Tanner was already in his car and driving away before she and Booker got to their cars.

"I thought he would help keep Veronica calm, but then maybe not," Judith said, thinking about Tanner's face when he found out Emma was missing. Then, turning to Booker, asked, "What's the plan?"

"I still need to find Walt. You go ahead and coordinate the search for Emma. Judith nodded and called Marsha to confirm the plan. The two of them agreed that Judith, April, and Cindy would search the town. Marsha would head the search in the woods with Daniel, Veronica, and Tanner, who were heading their way."

Margaret and Colin waited until the three of them had gone out the door, then walked to the window and watched them drive away.

"What do you think that's about?" Colin asked.

"Whatever it is, it's not good," Margaret replied. "We better get the town on our side, show them we are in charge, or we are both in deep trouble."

Turning to Colin, she added, "And don't you dare consider leaving town. You and I are going to turn this around together. If you leave, I will blame everything on you and send every authority I can find after you."

"I didn't kill Marshall. I wasn't the mastermind behind all the land grabs. That was you and Marshall, and I have proof. I won't leave town, but I will blame you if you turn on me."

Margaret's mood shifted without a beat. It was so quick that Colin found it creepy. After all the years of knowing Margaret, had he ever really known her? Watching her turn from terrifying to loving and concerned, he thought he hadn't. And now, he was probably in more trouble than he could ever have imagined.

His bluff worked, at least for the moment. But when Margaret realized that what he had said implicated him as much as her, she'd turn on him again because she would see him as weak enough to destroy. Perhaps it would be better to tell what he knew now. Or run. She wouldn't be able to find him, and then who cared if she blamed him for everything?

Colin knew Judith was like Margaret. Relentless. Eventually, she'd discover the truth. Margaret's career and grand plans would not survive once the truth came out. He didn't have to take revenge on her. Time would take care of that.

But he needed to protect himself. Run or tell. That was the question in front of him. Of course, he wouldn't be able to tell everything. Was it possible to keep hidden what needed to be hidden and still tell enough to get immunity?

Smiling at Margaret, who was now smiling at him, Colin didn't let any of his thoughts show. Instead, he followed Margaret's cue. For the rest of the afternoon, as they planned Marshall's funeral and spoke to the press, they both behaved as if they were allies, all the while knowing that they weren't. Both of them were sure that they were the one who would find a way out of the mess Marshall had created.

But both of them were wrong.

# Forty Four

T anner made it to The Ruby House, just as Daniel, Veronica, and Marsha were heading out the door. Slamming the car to a stop, he opened the door and ran at the three of them.

"Wait, I need to go too. Please, let me help."

Marsha barely knew who Tanner was, and thought they didn't need another person, but seeing Veronica's face as Tanner turned to her, said, "Okay, but you aren't dressed to go out into the woods."

Daniel, who had also seen how Tanner and Veronica looked at each other, realized Veronica wanted Tanner to come and said, "I have extra hiking stuff in my car. I think they'll fit."

As Tanner sat in Daniel's car trying on hiking boots, he whispered, "Thank you." Daniel nodded. He only wanted what was best for Veronica and Emma, and he could see that's what Tanner wanted too.

He recognized the signs. After all, it hadn't been that long since he had come to town and found Cindy, and probably everyone saw how he felt on his face long before he admitted it to himself. Maybe Tanner didn't know it yet, but he was in love with Veronica. If they weren't all so worried about Emma, he would clap this geeky accountant on the back and welcome him to their ever-growing family.

A few minutes later, the four of them piled into Marsha's SUV and headed to where they thought Emma must have entered the woods. Carrying flashlights in case it got dark while they were out there, they checked their phones to make sure they had service.

It was Daniel who pointed out the footsteps in the snow. They were melting and barely visible, but still possible to follow. Wasting no time, they all took off at a slow jog. There was no reason to separate. They were sure it was Emma's footsteps they were following.

It didn't take long for them to see where they were headed. In the distance, they could see the outline of buildings.

"The development," Marsha said. "She probably wanted more pictures."

"But then where is she?" Veronica wailed. "Our phones work out here. Why doesn't hers?"

No one answered because there was nothing they could say that would explain it. Within minutes they were all on the road, but there was so sign of Emma. As shocking as it was to find houses being built, and a road in the Green Zone, dealing with the implications of that was the last thing on their mind. All they wanted was to find Emma.

But there was no sign of her. The sun had warmed the road quicker than the ground, and all signs of footsteps had melted, leaving mostly slush and puddles of water.

"Where did she go?" Veronica cried. Tanner put his arms around her, and she slumped against him.

"Maybe she went into the houses," Daniel said, pointing to what looked like melted footsteps that led to the house closest to them. What they couldn't tell was if the footsteps were coming or going.

"How do we know if those are hers? What if someone else was here? Did she say she was meeting anyone here?" Marsha asked Tanner.

"She didn't."

The four of them stood for a moment, wondering if there had been someone else there. Worried. Was it a friend or foe? Had Emma known they were there?

"Well, it doesn't do us any good standing here trying to figure things out. Those could be her footsteps, and she could be in one of the houses," Marsha said, taking off at a run towards the first house.

Veronica, Daniel, and Tanner followed. When they didn't find her in the first house, they spread out to check on the rest of them. The houses were just shells with open walls waiting to be dry-walled, so it was easy to see that they were empty.

When they didn't find her, they met back inside the first house. Tanner kept his arm around Veronica who was shaking with cold and fear, all worry about hiding his feelings tossed aside.

"Well, she isn't here, and she didn't walk back the way she came or we would have seen her footsteps. So she must have followed the road," Daniel said. "So let's follow it ourselves and see where it goes."

Everyone nodded and started walking. Marsha called Judith to tell her what they had found and what they were doing.

No one mentioned that Emma probably would have done the same thing, if she could have. *But then Emma is still a teenager,* they said to themselves. *She might have wanted to solve the mystery first.*

It brought them a measure of comfort to think that.

Tanner's mind raced as they trudged forward. This development was smack in the middle of the protected Green Zone. And even though he had heard about it at the meeting, seeing it firsthand was shocking. But his primary concern was Emma. With every step they took, he kept an eye out for any sign of her—a dropped personal item, a footprint, a distinctive mark in the snow.

Every so often, a bird would chirp or the wind would rustle leaves, but aside from that, it was eerily silent. About a half a mile down the road, it split in two directions. The four of them stood for a minute, trying to decide which way to go. One way looked as if it might lead them back to town and the other deeper into the woods.

"I think I see something this way," Daniel said, gesturing to the road that led into the woods. Looking closely, they could see the outline of what looked like an old cabin, half hidden by tall trees and overgrown shrubs.

The group made their way towards it as quietly as possible. Deep in the woods, the sun hadn't melted the snow as much and they could see sets of footsteps leading to the cabin door.

Veronica's breath caught in her throat. "Those look fresh," she whispered. There were no lights on in the cabin, and not knowing what else to do, Daniel turned the rusty doorknob and then pushed the door open wider with his flashlight. They were met with a stale, musty smell. Inside, the small amount of light coming through the dirty window revealed a small living area with a sagging couch, a fireplace filled with ashes, and some discarded food wrappers.

A muffled noise came from the next room. The group froze. Tanner, arm still wrapped protectively around Veronica, cautiously moved forward.

"Emma?" he called out softly.

Another muffled sound, followed by a whimper. They rushed to the next room and found Emma tied to a chair, her mouth gagged. Her eyes widened in relief at seeing familiar faces.

Once the gag was removed, she whispered, "Someone grabbed me. I don't know who, but they left me here."

Veronica pulled her into a tight hug, tears streaming down both their faces. Tanner sighed with relief.

"We need to get out of here," Marsha said.

The group nodded in agreement. With Emma safely in their midst, they could figure out why and who later. It was getting dark. They needed to get back and get away in case Emma's assailant returned.

Flashlights on, they moved towards the road. Marsha called Judith and said they were taking a road that looked as if it was heading towards town. Judith said she could see where they were. She and Booker would find the entrance to the road and come to them. "Just keep moving," Judith said.

Behind a tree, staying out of the flashlight beam, a shadowy figure watched, eyes narrowing in anger and frustration. He knew he probably shouldn't have taken the girl, but seeing her taking pictures and videos, he lost his head for a moment.

The question was, what to do next? Run? Leave everything behind and just go? It was tempting. His time in Spring Falls had probably come to an end. But there were still a few people left to deal with. Then he'd go.

# Forty Five

Drained from her interactions with the group that discovered Emma, Judith made her way back home, calling Bruce on the way, saying she'd meet him there. Before leaving, she had made sure Emma felt safe in Tanner and Veronica's care. She had stayed long enough to hear Emma relay the day's events to Booker, but left when she realized there wasn't much more she could do at the moment.

Emma did not know who had attacked her. He hadn't spoken or shown her his face. He had grabbed her from behind and immediately slid what she assumed was a ski cap over her head.

Booker told Emma they'd talk the next day. Perhaps she'd remember more once she had rested. Everyone was exhausted. They'd start over again in the morning.

On her way home, Judith swung by the office to ensure that Nancy had rescheduled all her commitments for the coming day. As she drove, Judith silently berated herself. They were in the throes of tax season, and she was postponing meetings.

Although she had handed off the task of handling tax returns to her seasonal staff, she remained the bridge between them and the clients. But it was only mid-February, and everyone in town was in a tizzy over the two deaths, so she was getting away with it. For now.

Stripping off her wet coat and muddy shoes, Judith started towards the kitchen, but then pivoted and headed to the solace of her private bathroom attached to her office. This bathroom was her sanctuary. While there were other bathrooms in her house, this one was truly hers, complete with a luxurious soaking tub.

Filling the tub with water as hot as she could stand, she lit a few candles and settled into the steaming water. Slowly at first, and then, as she got used to it, sliding in the rest of the way with a sigh.

Laying her head back on the tub's cushioned edge, she thought through what had happened and what they had learned in the last few days. It didn't please her that she had been right when she had told Bruce months before that something was wrong in Spring Falls.

What would have been better was if she had identified the underlying issues before they spiraled into at least two deaths, unlawful developments, evictions, a missing council member, and Emma's frightening ordeal. Now everyone was aware of the turmoil. But the real puzzle remained. Who was orchestrating all this chaos? Who killed Marshall? Did Barbara die from the stress or something else? Where was Walt?

Margaret and the Town Council topped Judith's list of suspects behind the chaos. However, her history with Margaret made it hard to believe that the woman she grew up with could be involved in such terrible acts. Yes, Margaret had ambitions and was often ruthless, but was she more than that?

Judith's mind raced, weaving through the intricate web of Spring Falls' troubles. Yes, Margaret or Colin seemed to be the central figures in the problem, but weren't they innocent before proven guilty? But it was hard to ignore the fact that the Town Council members knew what Marshall was doing. And they had either taken part in or even instigated the illegal developments in town.

Colin, someone she had always seen as more of a follower than a leader, was now a suspect. But was it more than participating in the illegal activities? However, she found it hard to believe he would act alone.

And then there was Colin's cufflink. It seemed like a small yet significant piece of a much larger puzzle, given that the symbol was also in Marshall's painting. What did that symbol mean? She didn't have a clue other than confirming that Marshall and Colin were working together.

Judith thought again about Margaret's character. Was her ambition merely a veil for darker, more sinister motives? Judith could discern the hunger for power in Margaret's eyes. But was it so consuming that it could drive her to kill? Margaret had always been calculating, cold even, but to consider her capable of murder seemed a stretch.

Lingering in the warm water, Judith's thoughts kept turning over the possibilities. Was the Town Council collectively involved, or were there dissenting voices among them, voices silenced by coercion or by their deaths? Or could the Council be a pawn, manipulated by another hidden hand?

And what about Walt? His sudden disappearance was suspicious. Especially given his connection to the Town Council and what Tanner and Barbara had shared. Perhaps Walt wanted to be a whistleblower, and he was trying to escape the mess before it caught up to him. Or perhaps he too was a victim, silenced before he could reveal the truth.

The question of Colin and his misplaced cufflink continued to loom large in her mind. Could this seemingly incidental detail hold the key to the whole dire affair? A symbol—a link pointing to the truth? Judith felt a surge of resolve to pursue this idea and unearth any hidden implications.

And then there were the developments. Buildings springing up clandestinely in protected areas. Who stood to gain the most from this illegal expansion? The town's facade of tranquility and camaraderie was cracking. She could not let that continue. She needed to find answers quickly.

Judith's thoughts drifted to Tanner. She appreciated the way he had stepped up, especially concerning Veronica and Emma. There was a depth to him she hadn't seen before. The way he looked at Veronica was hard to ignore, and Judith hoped something good would come out of this chaos for the two of them.

As the water cooled, the weight of her unresolved questions grew heavier. The town was in turmoil, and she could feel the expectancy in the air. It was a collective hope that she would untangle the knots and restore normalcy.

Exhausted and filled with questions, she reluctantly left the comfort of the tub and dried off. She knew she needed to act swiftly and decisively. She needed to piece together the varied strands of information before the precarious balance of the town tipped over into more chaos.

Judith dressed and made her way to the living room, where Bruce was waiting, concern and support clear in his eyes. They needed to deliberate, to map out their next moves carefully. The unraveling fabric of Spring Falls needed mending, and they were at the epicenter of the storm, navigating through the debris of betrayal and greed.

Every question seemed to spawn more questions, and every answer seemed to deepen the shadows over the town. The path ahead was unclear, but Judith was determined. She would face the storm, unearth the truths buried under layers of deceit, and return Spring Falls to its former peaceful state.

Bruce smiled as Judith walked into the living room. Although her hair was wet, it still flared in the light. He knew her well. She was determined to get to the bottom of what was wrong in Spring

Falls, and he had found a document that might help her. Or it could make it worse, because it posed another question.

# Forty Six

Thursday morning dawned crisp and clear. Only various sizes of dirty gray snow piles beside roads and driveways remained. Looking out the window of the Ruby House, sipping their coffee, April and Marsha watched the town come alive.

There was nothing out of the ordinary. If they didn't know about Marshall and Barbara's deaths, illegal developments, Emma's ordeal in the cabin, or that Walt was missing, they would think they were starting another beautiful, quiet, and peaceful day in their beloved Spring Falls. But they knew that all that peace was hiding evil, and they had no idea what to do about it.

At the art gallery, Daniel, Cindy, Mimi, and Janet were doing the same thing. They were standing at the front window of the gallery staring out at the town, wondering how something so beautiful could hide so many bad things. How had that happened? When had it happened?

They had no answers to all their questions, so as they watched the town go by, each one wished the answers would simply walk down the street and reveal themselves. They needed answers so they could sort out the problems and then return to their normal lives.

Booker had asked all the Ruby Sisters and their extended family to keep an eye out for anything that seemed out of the ordinary, and that's what they were doing. But watching the town go by didn't seem very helpful. Everything looked as it always looked. What was wrong was still hidden, and that's how it had gone on for so long.

"Well," Cindy said, "We best get on with it."

The four of them were in the middle of uninstalling the last exhibit and installing the new one. They had a routine now. Each one knew their part, and the work flowed smoother each time they did it.

Later that day, Cindy was supposed to teach her art class—now one of her favorite things to do—but she had canceled it so they could all go to Marshall's funeral. And although they knew they had to go, they had mixed feelings about it.

They had always liked Marshall, but now it seemed wrong to have such a big event for someone who had likely sold out the town. But since they couldn't prove that, and most people weren't aware of the allegations, they had to go. There was always the slight chance that someone would give themselves away. Besides, they had once been friends with the man, and despite what he may have done, it had become a beautiful town, primarily under Marshall's watchful eye.

Just a few miles away, at Bree's house, Booker had just sat down to breakfast when his phone rang. Hanging up, he dropped his head, stared at his breakfast, and wondered if he could possibly eat anything.

Since the discovery of Marshall's body, his stomach had been tied up in knots, and every day it just got worse. They were no closer to understanding what had happened to Marshall. There were no clues.

Booker shook his head. How had being a small-town sheriff turned into this nightmare? Was he even capable of solving the mystery of Marshall's death or unraveling what appeared to be a web of illegal activities that Marshall must have been the head of?

It seemed obvious that someone wanted him dead because of what he had been doing. But why? And why now? What had changed? Did they know Marshall was leaving, and they'd be left with the mess he made?

So far, that was his best guess. And his best guess was that it was someone in the Town Council, but which one? And, of course, there were many people affected by what Marshall and his cronies had been up to, so there were many suspects, and he hadn't ruled out anyone yet.

But the phone call he had just received answered at least one question. He was grateful for that.

"What's wrong?" Bree asked.

"Barbara died of a heart attack."

"Oh, thank heavens. Not that she died. But, you know. That she wasn't killed like Marshall."

Booker nodded. "Yes, I am happy about that. So far, it doesn't look like someone is going around killing off Town Council members. But I still don't have any other answers. Marshall was very careful about what he was doing. Now it's all conjecture and allegations that he was behind the illegal developments.

"All the answers to what he was doing must have been on his computer. We found no documents at his house. Nothing. Marshall had made sure his house was empty of anything that incriminated him. His killer either lucked out, or waited for that moment, knowing all he needed to take was the computer."

Bree stood behind Booker, rubbing his shoulders, wondering who she would make the villain if she were writing this in a book. There were too many possibilities, and many of them they didn't even know about yet.

"Have you searched Barbara's house? Maybe she had records."

"Yes. And she had some. Judith is looking through them. Hopefully, there will be some information we can use to find out who killed Marshall."

"What about the people building the developments in the Green Zone? Or who is making Pedro and his friends leave their homes? Wouldn't they be suspect too?"

"Of course, but so far, we don't know who they are. Everyone working on the developments work for shell companies. We haven't gotten to the actual owners yet. All we could do so far was stop all construction and evictions, which is good news for Pedro and his friends.

"We also got permission to audit Margaret, Colin, and Walt's books last night. Judith and Tanner will start on them today."

"Sounds promising," Bree said. "That is, if they have only one set of books. Which is unlikely."

"Agreed. And that could lead us back to knowing nothing."

"What time is Marshall's funeral?"

"Noon. For some reason, that was Marshall's favorite time of the day, or so Margaret said. And of course, she is turning it into a big event. She needs to be seen as in charge."

"Do you think she is responsible for what happened to Marshall?"

Booker shook his head. "I don't know. I wish I did."

# Forty Seven

Neither Bruce nor Judith had slept well, both of them wondering if what Bruce had learned from a client had anything to do with Marshall's death. Judith couldn't see how it fit in. It was just one more thing that they hadn't known about Marshall. He had been married, divorced, and had a son. But maybe it mattered that Margaret had known. That's what Bruce's client had told him anyway. If Margaret knew about the son, did she know who he was?

Still, they had called Booker and told him, and he promised to get someone looking for an ex-wife and son immediately. If nothing else, it would delay doing anything with Marshall's estate.

"The son couldn't have killed his father for his estate, could he?" Bruce had asked. The three of them had agreed it was possible, but who was the son? Why hadn't he made himself known before? Did they know him? Had Marshall known him and didn't tell anyone?

The only thing they knew was that the son would be about Tanner's age. Other than that, there was nothing. But despite a missing ex-wife and son, the three of them thought that Marshall's murder probably had to do with the illegal activities that Marshall had been carrying on for years. Activities that could have begun when Judith had worked for him all those years ago.

For Judith, that thought always made her feel guilty. Yes, she had been young and didn't know much when she went to work for Marshall. But what if she had paid more attention? Could she have stopped him? What would the town be like if he hadn't been mayor?

However, despite what they now knew about him, it was difficult to imagine Spring Falls without Marshall as mayor. Because no matter what else he had done, there was no denying that he had improved the town. For most people.

There was another reason Judith couldn't sleep. Bruce had asked her a question she didn't want to answer. He wanted to know what she thought would happen to the town once it was clear that the Town Council had been involved in the illegal developments. Who would keep the town together then? How could the town survive when all its top officials went to jail?

It was a question that Bruce said needed to be answered. And soon. Because it was only a matter of time before they had proof of who had been involved, and he was sure that Margaret, Colin, and Walt were not innocent. Either they only took part, or one of them was the leader. Either way, they were guilty.

Bruce had told Judith what he thought would work to save the town and asked her to do it. And she had immediately said no. She had never, ever wanted to be a politician. Ever.

Bruce replied that a politician wasn't what the town needed. They needed a leader, and she was the obvious choice. Almost everyone in town already knew her, and whether or not they agreed with her about issues, they admired who she was. She stood for integrity. Something Spring Falls would need in a leader more than anything else.

She would not have to change and be someone else. She would remain Judith, with the hair that flamed when something was wrong. That's what the town needed.

Holding her hands as she looked away, Bruce said that the solution to keeping the town from falling apart would be her running for mayor. She could then put together a Town Council that could be trusted. She could fix the problems caused by the current administration, and then, if she wanted to, she could step down.

"Will you do it?" Bruce had asked.

Judith had said no, no, no, over and over again to herself and then to Bruce, even though in her heart she knew he was right. Who else could step up and save the town? So, although she had said no, she hadn't stopped thinking about it.

And when she kissed Bruce goodbye that morning as he left for his office, she had whispered, "Maybe," and he had known what she meant.

But that was the future. Now. she had work to do. On her desk lay Barbara's files, and she was hoping to get answers from them about who was behind the chaos. And perhaps they contained something that would help them find who killed Marshall and stole his computer.

The possibility that Barbara's papers would reveal who had participated in the illegal activities had also kept Judith awake. Finally, long before dawn, she had gotten up to get to work, hoping to find out who all had been part of Marshall's circle.

Folders and papers were piled on her desk along with Colin's cufflink. She kept it in front of her, hoping it would tell her something. So far, it hadn't sparked a single idea. Just because the symbol matched the one Marshall had asked Cindy to put in his painting didn't have to mean anything other than the obvious—that the two of them had been working together, and that they both liked hidden power and control. That was already so obvious, Judith didn't think it deserved any more of her attention.

She'd take the cufflink to Colin and give it back to him at the funeral. Booker had already given her permission to do so. They had everything they needed to find it again if they needed to.

Sifting through Barbara's files, Judith couldn't find anything that stood out. Most of the papers were about her nursery business. Barbara had said she hadn't been involved in what the rest of the Council had been doing. She just didn't turn them in. And so far, everything Judith found seemed to agree with that. Barbara wasn't guilty of doing something wrong, but she wasn't innocent either. She had turned a blind eye to what was happening.

On the other hand, Barbara had finally come forward, and Judith hoped Barbara had found some peace in knowing she had done the right thing in the end.

As she organized Barbara's files for Bruce so he could help her son settle Barbara's estate, she noticed that one folder had an old photograph of the members of the Town Council. They were standing in front of City Hall. In it, a much younger Colin stood beside Marshall. Walt was beside Colin, and Marshall had his arm around Margaret. Barbara was in it too, a little off to the side, looking uncomfortable. The back of the photo had a date, and a scribbled note she recognized written in what she recognized as Marshall's unruly handwriting. "To our prosperous future."

Chills ran down Judith's spine. Someone had drawn a crude representation of the triangle, eye, and vine. All of this had started so long ago. If only Barbara had spoken up then.

Still, she had no proof. What she needed was Marshall's computer. Find that, they'd find the killer and whoever else was involved in the coverup.

Glancing at her watch, Judith realized the morning was almost gone, and the funeral was just an hour away. She couldn't believe that it was happening so soon, and was going to be such an enormous affair. But that was Margaret, always going for the chance to be in front of the public.

Booker had asked them all to be there. Maybe someone would do or say something that would help them find answers. As Judith quickly changed into something appropriate for a February funeral, her resolve strengthened. Even though she had no proof, it felt to her as if they were getting closer to solving both crimes, the murder, and the illegal activities. And there was always the chance that Walt would show up, and just say he had taken a few days off, and he would tell them everything they needed to know to prove what had happened.

*Dream on*, she said to herself. Walt's disappearance was disturbing. Did he leave on purpose, or did someone take him? She had to hope he had simply taken time to decide what to do, but she knew that probably that wasn't what had happened.

# Forty Eight

The funeral was packed, just as Margaret had intended it to be. She had made sure everyone in town knew when it was, and even if they weren't invited, they would watch the news. And as planned, she stood out. She made sure that the press, as agreed, had their cameras on her as much as possible.

During the eulogy, she cried just enough to be seen as having a heart, but not so much that she looked weak. Instead, she was the strong and capable woman who had always stood by Marshall's side and now, of course, would continue his legacy.

She gracefully wove into the eulogy the fact that it had been less than a week between the celebration of Marshall's life as the Mayor, to this honoring of the man who had made the town the beautiful, safe, and peaceful place that they all loved. His death was a tragedy, and she would make sure someone paid for taking away their beloved mayor.

It was perfection, and Margaret knew it. She had the town crying and feeling sorry for her while wanting her to lead them into the future. It was a gift, one that Margaret did not take lightly. She practiced. She had hired coaches and trainers. Not from town, though. Never someone local. She couldn't have it appear as if what she did wasn't effortless.

Conferences and trainings had always given her the excuse to get out of town, where she would spend early evenings socializing as was expected of her. But then she would meet whatever expert she had hired in the hotel room and do the work. A lot of it.

If someone saw people coming to her room and thought she was having affairs, it wouldn't matter. That was to be expected. That she was training herself would not be as accepted or approved of. Especially because she was a woman.

At the thought of all the work she had put into becoming the master of any room, Margaret smiled to herself while gritting her teeth against the unfairness of the world that always put men in charge and on a pedestal. Most of them were bumbling fools.

Except Marshall, who had also put in the work to become the man that he was. But being a man studying to be a better orator or leader was admired. Still, it wasn't his fault that he was a man. Marshall had believed in her, and she would forever be grateful to him. She knew it was entirely possible to be grateful to her mentor and, at the same time, be glad that he was gone.

His death paved the way nicely to her next goal. She had always intended to knock all the men who thought they were in charge off of their righteous stances. Spring Falls was just the beginning. A few years as mayor, then governor, then the ultimate prize.

But she couldn't give any of those plans away just yet. Today, and until they elected her mayor, she would give the people of Spring Falls whatever they wanted. The people needed to relate to her, and that meant a lot of listening, and then saying the exact right thing at the exact right time. But she had trained for this moment. She was ready.

Watching Margaret, Colin could feel the anger that always burned deep within his gut start to flare up. She was working the room, stealing the show, making herself out to be the savior of the town. And he finally admitted to himself what he had tried to ignore for years. They had never been a team. None of them had.

When Marshall was alive, they had all agreed that he was the leader. Of course he was. He had the plans. He had the know-how. Marshall had the hearts of everyone in town. Almost everyone loved and admired him. Only a few dissenters spoke out against him each year when he ran for mayor.

No one really listened to anyone who opposed the mayor. Why would they? Each year, the town prospered. Colin knew that even if people had suspected that the mayor was doing side deals, they wouldn't have cared, as long as it didn't affect them, and they had a safe, beautiful town to live in. If someone was suffering for it, as long as they didn't know about it, or it didn't affect them, they would ignore it.

All of them had taken advantage of Marshall's popularity. And Colin thought they all had agreed that they were equal under his rule. But now he had to fully accept that it hadn't been true. Margaret had never intended to share anything. He had been duped. He was Margaret's lackey, her boy-toy, the go-to guy who did the dirty work while she took all the credit.

While Margaret stood in front of the town declaring herself Marshall's chosen one, not once had she turned to him to bring him into the limelight with her. Colin saw it so clearly now. He had been used. They all had, but what did he care about them? It was time for it to be all about him.

Watching Margaret at work, Colin felt as if all that he had done had been worthless. What had he gotten out of it? A little popularity. Money. Yes, but it hadn't been enough.

Until that moment, watching Margaret, Colin had not fully understood how much he had wanted to be the one that people admired and looked up to. After all, he was the one who had done so much of Marshall's work behind the scenes. But of course, he couldn't get the glory for that. It had to be Margaret who simply gave orders and expected them to be carried out.

As on the night of Marshall's retirement party, Colin's anger now expanded and a red haze folded over him. He knew that feeling. He knew it was the kind of anger that caused wars, and in his own family, had made his father such a bully and tyrant that Colin had barely survived. Usually, he could contain the anger. He would let it simmer, but never burn hot. But today, he would not tamp it down. Instead, he was going to use it.

Slipping away from the funeral was easy. No one cared that he was there. All eyes were on Marshall's casket and Margaret standing beside it, acting as the appointed guardian both for Marshall's legacy and the future of Spring Falls.

*We'll see about that,* Colin said to himself. He may never be the mayor of Spring Falls, but his bags were already packed to go somewhere warm and sunny where he'd be unknown and happy. He had enough money to last many lifetimes. Let the town fall apart. It didn't matter in the slightest to him.

But before he left, he'd let the red haze fuel him like never before, and he'd make sure that Marshall and Margaret, and all the rest of the people involved, would fall off the pedestals that the town had put them on.

The town thought they were safe from people like him, and yet all along he had been there, along with the others who didn't give a rat's ass about the town. They were there for the power and the money. At least he had been. And he now would do something that would hurt them all.

Slipping out the back door, he made the phone call to put his plans into action. Getting into his car, already packed to go, he was finally happy. He was cleaning up the mess they had made. The plans had been in place. He just hadn't been ready before. Now he was.

On the other end of the phone, Leon Price laughed. "You crazy bastard. Sounds fun."

Leon hung up, checked his bank account to make sure Colin had transferred the money, and headed to the developments. The girl had been rescued, so he wasn't worried about her now. Instead, every development would burn. One last job for Colin, and then it was time for him to leave town, too.

# Forty Nine

Margaret was heading to the back of the church in order to shake people's hands as they exited, when she first smelled the smoke. At first she thought she was smelling fireplace smoke. There were a few people in town who used wood to heat their homes.

But then someone else asked, "Do you smell smoke?"

The crowd paused for a split second, before people started rushing to the door. Booker's cell phone rang. Glancing at the message, he stepped up to the podium and spoke through the microphone, "Don't panic, it's not this building."

The crowd looked back at him, but stopped only for a moment before continuing to push their way out the open door.

Booker knew they were wondering, even if it wasn't this building, where was it? Why was the smoke smell so strong?

At that moment, the fire alarm rang throughout the town. The crowd paused for a moment before pushing even harder to get out the door. Booker yelled, "Let us through." Finally, the crowd moved aside to let Booker and half of the men in the church out the door. Everyone knew where they were going.

Spring Falls had a few permanent firefighters, but most of the squad was comprised of volunteers. And most of those volunteers were at Marshall's funeral service.

Within minutes, the church was empty. Outside, those that weren't heading to the fires stood frozen in place. It seemed impossible, but there were plumes of smoke rising into the clear blue sky from every direction.

Judith stood outside with all the Ruby Sisters, shivering in the winter wind, trying to decide where they could be the most help. Glancing back through the open doors into the chapel, Judith noticed that Margaret had walked back to Marshall's casket and was standing alone beside it. *His burial would have to be another day.* Judith thought it was one of the saddest things she had ever seen. Margaret and Marshall together. No longer the center of attention.

Margaret looked up to see Judith watching her and smiled. She couldn't let that woman see how affected she was by the destruction of her plans to be seen as the savior of the town. Leading Marshall's procession to the cemetery would have been the highlight of the day.

But here she was, alone, and there was Judith, surrounded by friends. She stood next to the one man she had related to, and now he was gone. And even though she hadn't looked outside to see where the fires were, she already knew.

What they had built together was burning.

"I'm sorry, Marshall," she whispered to the casket, and then turned and walked away. Away from the people standing at the front of the chapel. Away from her plans. It was time to make new plans.

However, as she walked, she thought about what she was giving up if she walked away and realized she didn't want to. She wanted what she had always wanted, and this was only a minor setback. She could fix it. And she thought she knew exactly what to do. It was a Hail-Mary pass, but she might be able to pull it off. If anyone could do it, it would be her.

But there wasn't much time. Whoever spoke first would win, and that meant she would have to hurry. Turning back, she placed a call to have the camera crew meet her in the chapel. She would stand again beside Marshall's casket and reveal who had set the fires and who killed Marshall.

Booker and his team were busy. She'd be in charge while they tried to put out fires. All she had to do was convince everyone that what she told them was true. And since some of it was, that shouldn't be too hard.

They'd believe her because they wanted to believe it. No one wanted to believe that she and Marshall had orchestrated what had now turned into chaos. They would willingly accept that it was someone else. And she'd hand them that person on a platter. Signed, sealed, and delivered. It would be close enough to the truth to be the truth.

She could still keep the hearts and minds of Spring Falls and keep all her plans in place. This is what she had trained herself to do. She would put on the performance of her life. Lie, lie, lie and keep on lying. Anything that didn't agree with her lies would be fake news. She knew it would work. It worked in the big picture. It would certainly work in a small town that wanted to believe her.

She stopped in the church restroom to check her makeup and hair. Thinking she looked a little too perfect, she messed it up just enough to look as if this tragedy had affected her.

It had. Just not in the way anyone would think or be willing to believe.

# Fifty

argaret's performance was magnificent. She began her press conference standing beside the casket. Then she moved outside, where she angled herself so there was smoke and fire behind her while she promised the residents of Spring Falls that she would find the person responsible and make sure they were punished for their crimes.

Because she hinted she knew who it was, the press wouldn't leave her alone. They pushed and prodded, demanding answers. After much equivocating, she finally gave them enough hints that the press decided she must mean that it was Colin Parker.

"Was it Colin Parker?" They shouted at her. Not answering the question directly, she added, "He probably had help if it was."

It was a crazy thing to do, and Margaret knew it. If she were wrong, she was finished. But she didn't think she was, and she was pretty sure she knew who had helped him.

The frenzy of questions thrown at her after that announcement was just what Margaret wanted. It was okay because she was positive it was Colin. After all, she had pushed him into it. Knowing that, it buoyed her assurance to the crowd.

She had seen Colin's face when she had given him no attention or credit during her eulogy for Marshall. She had ignored him on purpose. Margaret knew his temper. And she hoped she could tip him over the edge to do something irrevocably stupid in public. And she had. She had watched him slip out of the church, and when she saw the fires, she knew it had to be him who had set them. It wasn't exactly what she expected him to do, but she could make it work.

And, of course he couldn't have set all those fires on his own so quickly. Colin would have called Leon Price, the man who often did Colin's dirty work. Margaret considered it ironic that Leon owned a cleaning company, knowing that there were many kinds of cleaning up that Leon did. Especially for Colin.

Leon was a piece of work. Charming, cool, and utterly without a moral compass. She thought that Leon's last name of Price fit him perfectly. He had a price for everything.

Margaret knew exactly when Colin and Leon had met. She had been having lunch with Colin when a nice-looking young man had come over to their table and introduced himself. That was another thing about Leon. He was not shy about promoting himself. He used his good looks to his advantage. Leon had the kind of smile that made you want to smile back, even though you weren't sure you could trust him.

That day, Leon had explained that he was new in town, had heard that Colin was the premier real estate broker in town, and he wanted to introduce himself. Leon had told them both that his goal was to have the company that every real estate agent used to clean homes before they were sold.

Colin had taken to Leon immediately, treating him like the son he never had. With Colin's help and backing, it didn't take long for Leon's dream to come true. Within a few years, it was Leon's company that almost everyone called to clean up after events or parties. His company was also the choice of many businesses in town to clean their buildings after work. Leon's crews were everywhere.

That happened not only because of Colin's help. It was Leon himself. He was a natural. Within months, Leon knew almost everyone in town, and everyone knew of him. Watching Leon work a room, Margaret had thought that, in his own way, Leon was a lot like Marshall. He easily won hearts and minds. And he was a natural businessman, learning quickly from mistakes and shifting directions as needed.

But despite all that, Margaret couldn't say she knew much about Leon. He was a public figure, but a very private person. The only personal thing she knew about him was that his mother had died and he had come to town, looking to start a new life with the money his mother had left him. He had never mentioned a father, so she had to assume that he was not in the picture.

Colin had continued to support Leon, and their relationship had matured into good friends and business partners. Colin was a stuck-up, arrogant prick who could appear nice when he wanted to, but Leon was comfortable with him, and Colin seemed to genuinely care for Leon.

In some ways, they were the same. They were both masters at manipulating the public's attention and using it to their advantage. Margaret had admired them both for that ability. After all, it was her and Marshall's specialty, too.

It didn't mean she liked and trusted them though, and given that they had brought this mess on themselves, she had no hesitation in throwing them both under the bus. Her guess was that they would never be found, so they would not care in the long run about what she did. She assumed they had set the fires and left town, leaving her free to blame them for everything. In the end, she'd blame them for Marshall's death, too.

As she acted out the role of her life, Margaret quietly thanked herself for becoming the kind of woman who knew how to set up this scenario in advance to her advantage. No, it hadn't gone exactly as planned. But it was close enough.

She could make it work.

# Fifty One

What Margaret didn't count on was Judith's immediate and decisive reaction to what she was doing. Judith had watched the press conference with distrust, looking for cracks in Margaret's story. She watched Margaret point the blame for the fires at Colin and Leon. Although on the surface, Margaret appeared distressed over what she was saying, Judith detected a gleam of satisfaction.

Of course, Judith knew Colin and Leon. Everyone did. And yes, she believed that they could have started the fires. But did they?

By pointing the press to Colin and Leon, Margaret was removing herself from any blame, while still keeping the attention on her. It was true Margaret. Judith had watched Margaret do this kind of thing since they were kids.

Margaret always found a way to take a kernel of truth and make it the whole thing, so even if what she was saying was a lie, it sounded true to undiscerning ears. Judith was sure that Margaret was setting the stage to wiggle out of any blame when the town found out what the Council had been up to. Even though

Judith knew it was Margaret who held the reins of the Council in partnership with Marshall, it might be hard to prove.

Judith thought it was entirely possible that it was Margaret who had pushed Marshall down the stairs and stolen his computer. It would leave the field wide open to taking the power she always wanted, while making sure no one knew what she had been up to.

Booker had already ordered a search of Margaret's home and office to look for Marshall's computer. But Judith doubted they'd find anything. If Margaret had had it, she would have destroyed it. But knowing Margaret, she would have kept a backup of it somewhere. It was easy enough to hide thumb drives.

Watching Margaret, Judith felt foolish for not having really seen Margaret for who she was long ago. But she was going to see her with fresh eyes, as someone who had been taking the town on her own ride for years.

However, even if Margaret didn't have the computer, Judith was glad that Booker was searching Margaret's home and office. They needed to find something, anything. Even the smallest incriminating evidence about something Margaret had done wrong in order to get people to look in the right direction. Margaret's direction.

And now that Judith was willing to admit she had missed what had been happening in Spring Falls, she was sure that all the chaos in town resulted from the alliance between Margaret and Marshall. Margaret could cast the blame on others, but Judith knew they would eventually discover Margaret was the key to the mess that Spring Falls was now in.

But Booker was busy at the moment, like most of the men in town, fighting the fires. Judith thought was probably the point of the fires. With everyone's attention on the emergency, it would give all the people responsible a chance to escape.

Judith's hair flared. It was going to be up to her, with help from the Ruby Sisters, to find out the truth of what Margaret and

Marshall had done. The question was where to look. She had gone through all of Barbara's papers, but had found nothing.

Bruce's discovery that Marshall had once been married and had a son might be helpful. But how would they find the son? And even if they did, would he know anything? However, it was a thread they would have to pull. Maybe it would point them towards more information.

The problem was they knew nothing about him. They didn't know where he lived, or even what name he was going by. Did he use his mother's last name, or invent one of his own? Did he look like his mother, or Marshall? And since they didn't know what his mother looked like, if he did look like her, that wouldn't help, anyway.

The woman had vanished within months of marrying Marshall, taking their newborn son with her. Judith wondered if both of them were still alive. Was Marshall above having them killed? Or did the person who killed him also kill his family years before?

*How long has this evil been going on in Spring Falls?* Judith asked herself, And how stupid she had been for not noticing.

When she had worked for Marshall, there was no evidence that he had ever been married. His marriage had been over and done with by the time he was twenty. Marshall had hidden that part of his life well.

Judith wondered if maybe that failed marriage was what pushed him into being a mayor. Was it heartbreak that had fueled Marshall, or a desire to serve, or what now appeared to be greed for money and power? If she would have been a little wiser at twenty, she might have been able to stop the whole thing before it started.

But even now, she wasn't much smarter. Thinking through what she knew, it amazed Judith how little she knew about Marshall. After all, for over forty years, he had been the public figurehead for Spring Falls. But what had they known about his personal life? Did Marshall ever look for his wife and son? Did he find them? Or did he already know what had happened to them?

Working with Matt, Judith's expertise in finding things on the internet. Bruce had already started a search for both Marshall's ex-wife and son. But it could take days to get an answer. Besides, did it have any bearing on Marshall's death or what was happening now?

All Judith had were questions with no answers, but she thought perhaps they would get some if they found Walt. Judith didn't believe that he was dead. She thought he was probably hiding out somewhere. But where?

Judith turned to the Ruby Sisters, who had been standing next to her watching her think, and waiting for what she would ask them to do.

"While Margaret is busy painting herself the heroine of Spring Falls, let's find Walt."

"What about Colin and Leon?" Bree asked. "She's implying that they are the ones who set the fires. Shouldn't we find them too?"

Judith smiled as she answered.

"I expect they are both already in jail at the police station, or will be soon. Booker had them watched. They won't get far."

"Both of them? Even Leon?" Cindy asked. "Why would they watch Leon?"

"It's public knowledge how much Colin counted on Leon. If he had needed something done, he would have called Leon to help him."

"That makes little sense, then," Bree said. "If they were being watched, how could they have set the fires?"

"Right," Judith said. "That's why it's unlikely that it was them."

"Which is why you want to find Walt," Marsha said.

"But I thought he was the whistleblower," Cindy said.

"Maybe setting the fires is how he is blowing the whistle," April responded.

Judith nodded. "Exactly. So how do we find him?"

In the end, it was Walt who found them.

# Fifty Two

Walt stared at the phone, trying to decide whether to make the call. Would he have the balls to finally do what was right, or was he still too chicken-hearted to act? Leave or stay? He had been debating that question for hours. No one knew where he was, so it would be entirely possible to get away from this mess and start over.

He had finally done something. Lit up the town, so to speak. Now, no one could ignore what had been happening. Was he required to do more than that? Didn't setting the fires make up for what had come before and what he did and didn't do?

In his heart, Walt knew it didn't. He'd never be completely innocent. Almost. Not quite. Maybe he had never been. He, like so many others, had fallen prey to the siren of wanting more.

Even when he realized what had happened and tried to turn back, he had waited too long to act. Then guilt and shame took over, and he couldn't think straight. The spiraling mess he had made of his life was entirely his fault. He could have said no.

The guilt that still plagued him was why he was staring at the phone, trying to decide if he had to place a call or not. Trying to decide what kind of man he was, or perhaps could be if he would just make that phone call.

Days before, Walt had destroyed his own phone, so no one could track him. Then he had hidden in plain sight. In the basement of his bookstore, there was a room where he kept all the rare books. In the 1950s, the owners had built it as a bomb shelter. He had stocked the room just in case. For the past few days, he had been hiding there, reading rare books and trying to build up his courage. He came out only at night to breathe clean air and to get more food.

*Just like a vampire,* he thought. And like a vampire, he and the Town Council had been sucking the lifeblood out of Spring Falls.

Now, this phone was his only chance to do the next right thing. But did he have the courage to make the call? Walt didn't know. He could simply use the store's phone, but he didn't want them to know where he was calling from. Just in case he decided to run after all.

The phone in his hand was the last one he had out of the packs of burner phones that Marshall had given all of them when they were doing Marshall's business. Make a call, throw it away, had been the rule. Underneath the kind-hearted act Marshall had shown the town, had been a mean, vindictive, and distrustful man.

Walt thought Marshall had been the perfect villain. Not too charming. Not too perfect so that people would question if he had a heart. Marshall allowed himself to make public mistakes, and then he would publicly quickly correct them. People ate it up. It had made Walt feel sick to his stomach all the time.

To see how Marshall manipulated the world, you had to know him well. And apparently no one cared to look too closely. After all, most of the town got what they wanted. Marshall was brilliant. Even more than Margaret knew. She had thought she was in charge when she never was. It had always been Marshall.

But Walt knew Marshall had what seemed to him to be a fatal flaw. Marshall believed everyone was someone who could be swayed or bought by, greed, power, or money. Marshall assumed everyone had a price, and he would meet it.

And if they couldn't be bought, he could count on their apathy or fear. Barbara was the perfect example. She knew what was going on, but did nothing about it until it was too late. Walt hoped that as Barbara died, she had forgiven herself. He knew how hard it was to stand up to people like Marshall.

*How can I be mad at her or blame her for her inaction?* Walt thought. *I knew. I participated. And even when I discovered it wasn't worth it, I did nothing until Tanner came into the Council and I saw my chance to get out from under Marshall and Margaret's rules.*

Which brought Walt back to the question of what to do next. If he turned himself in, he had enough information to bring all the Town Council's activities to light. But by doing so, he would also condemn himself to prison, because he was not innocent. He had participated. He had made money.

But what he had done had not made him happy. After his wife died, he had been so lonely that he would have given everything he had to have time again with her. Instead of trying to be somebody, he would have chosen to be her husband first. He had no one. What good would the money he made do him now if he ran? Ran from what to what? What good had he done in the world?

Maybe now was his chance to do something the right way. Although Walt didn't believe that people hung around after death, for a moment he felt a warm wave rush through him and he imagined his wife's voice telling him it was the right decision and she was proud of him.

He knew he had imagined it, but it was enough to tip him over the edge. He'd call Tanner. This was a young man with a future.

Someone who had already started to uncover what the Council had been doing and then reported it to Judith.

Tanner was Marshall and Margaret's biggest mistake. They thought they could buy him, but they were wrong. And they were wrong about Walt too in the long run. He could stand up to them. He deserved to pay for what he had done, or not done, to protect people from Marshall's plan.

When Tanner answered the phone, Walt started to cry.

After a long pause, Tanner asked, "Are you at the bookstore?"

Taking a deep breath, Walt answered, "Yes. Could you come here with Judith?"

"It will be alright, Walt," Tanner had replied.

While he waited, Walt clung to that idea. It would be alright.

# Fifty Three

Smoke thickened the air, making each breath Colin took feel like a lungful of sandpaper. He clutched at the mask he'd snatched from his car, pressing it to his face. Everywhere he looked, others were masked too, remnants from the days of Covid. But this time, they were warding off the bite of the smoke, not a virus. Colin grimaced, wondering if these masks, barely adequate now, had truly been any barrier during the pandemic.

With every turn he made, the fire seemed to greet him. The first development was already ablaze before he got there. He hadn't even struck a single match. Was Leon already on the move before their call? A jarring ringtone cut through his spiraling thoughts. It was Leon, his voice full of fury and disbelief. "I thought this was my gig!" Leon spat.

"It wasn't me!" Colin's voice was muffled by the mask, distorted further by the car's interior. He found himself shouting just to be heard.

A string of curses, and then silence. Leon had hung up. Panic and confusion danced in Colin's head. If neither of them had lit the fires, then who did? But there was nothing he could do now except keep driving and get out of town and then out of the country as fast as he could. Once he was safe, he'd find out. Or maybe not. Maybe he would just walk away from it all and never look back.

But a piercing wail broke through his chain of thoughts—sirens. Glancing in the rearview mirror, the flashing blue and red lights were unmistakable. With a heavy sigh, Colin pulled over. It was time to rely on his gift of gab to navigate out of this mess.

The air in the police station was thick with tension. Leon's face, already hard from past confrontations, tightened further when Colin was ushered in. Their eyes met, but no words were exchanged.

Colin's gaze darted around, noting the layout and the exits. But his heart sank when he spotted Judith in deep conversation with Sheriff Booker. If there was anyone more formidable than Margaret, it was Judith. Her piercing intelligence and instincts had an uncanny way of unraveling even the most tightly wound plans.

To Colin's shock, she simply acknowledged him and Leon with a curt nod before sweeping out of the room. Her departure only intensified the brewing storm of questions in Colin's mind.

"Why am I here?" he blurted out, instantly regretting the edge in his voice. It wasn't the right tone to take if he wanted to get out of this mess.

Booker, cool and inscrutable, didn't even afford him a full glance. He whispered something to an officer, and with a curt nod, headed out.

Colin's anxiety intensified. On the other side of the room, Leon's face mirrored his own feelings. Their meticulously laid plans were unraveling fast, and the silence of the station was only amplifying their fears.

What was happening? A TV in the room's corner showed them that the fires were almost out. Masses of dark smoke were rising from what was left of the development.

Now everyone in town would know that someone had been building in the Greenbelt. And eventually, they would find proof of who had been doing it. Colin wondered how anyone of them were going to get out of this mess.

An hour went by while he and Leon sat squirming in their chairs, trying not to even look at each other. And then Booker returned with Margaret. She flinched when she saw the two of them still sitting in the waiting room, as if they were just there for an appointment.

Still not speaking, Booker pointed to a chair, and Margaret huffed over and sat down.

Her voice, steady but cold, broke the room's silence. "Lawyer."

Booker's reaction was nonchalant, a simple lift of his shoulders. But the mood shifted once again as another officer entered, taking a position by the door. The message was clear. They weren't going anywhere.

Margaret wondered who or what they were waiting for. But the delay gave her time to steady her thoughts. She looked over at Leon and Colin and gave them a look intended to scare the bejesus out of both of them.

A moment of terror ran through her when Colin stared back and Leon lifted a middle finger before he too looked away. But then she remembered she wasn't guilty. At least not on paper. No one could prove anything.

Except maybe Walt. But he was missing. For now, she was safe. And now that she knew she was on her own, she would make sure all the blame shifted away from her and onto everyone else. After all, she had proof of what Marshall had been doing, and she had made sure none of it pointed back to her.

She would plead innocent, and she was sure that she would get away with it. Spinning in her chair so she was staring at both Leon and Colin, she let herself relax. If she could imagine herself as being anything, it was a snake. Calm and collected in the heat, she'd only strike when she was good and ready.

Leon and Colin would go down in flames just as the developments had. Whoever had set those fires might have done her a favor, although she was sure that was not what they had intended. It didn't matter. She knew what she had to do. Her only worry was Walt. Where was he, and whose side was he on? Perhaps he had already left the country, and that would eliminate that problem.

When the door opened and Walt walked in, followed by Judith and Tanner, her heart sank. Based on the look on Walt's face, none of them had a chance of escaping what they had done.

# Fifty Four

"But who killed Marshall?" April's voice broke the tense silence. She sat huddled next to the fireplace in Judith's living room, seeking warmth from the crackling flames.

Outside, a frigid wind howled, causing the tree branches to clatter against each other. Although snow threatened to blanket the town again, it hadn't deterred the Ruby Sisters and their circle of friends from gathering at Judith's once again. They needed answers.

It had taken a few days to get the entire Town Council, except Tanner, arrested and booked. More arrests would be forthcoming. Builders and contractors who had been on Marshall's payroll topped the list.

Given all that had happened, very few details had been leaked. It was going to be a public mess, and everyone had agreed to keep it quiet as long as possible until they had ironed out solutions on how to run the town.

Booker gazed around the room, taking in his friends' concerned faces. This wasn't just about damage control. It was about rebuilding trust. The people in Judith's living room weren't just spectators. They were integral to the path forward for Spring Falls. Spring Falls would need them more than ever.

So now, on a cold and dark Friday night, they were all gathered together to get answers. They needed to know enough so that they could plan the town's rebuilding.

Barely breathing, the entire room waited for Booker's answer to April's question.

So even though Booker said it quietly, everyone heard.

"His son."

There was an audible gasp, and then everyone started talking at once. But it was Marsha who spoke the loudest and asked the obvious question.

"His son? Since when did Marshall have a son? And who is it?"

Marsha sat next to Cindy on the couch, with Daniel beside Cindy on her other side. His arm was draped behind Cindy, pulling her close. Eager to catch every word from Booker, Marsha leaned towards him as much as she could.

Before speaking, Booker paused, his gaze methodically sweeping across the crowded room, making eye contact with each individual in Judith's packed living room. He didn't want to leave anyone out of this discussion.

Tanner, Veronica, and Emma sat on the other couch, the three of them looking like a family. Booker had the happy thought that it hadn't taken long for them to bond. That was good. Tanner was going to need a lot of support. As the only remaining member of the Town Council, everything was going to get thrown at him. It was going to be a heavy responsibility.

Booker looked over at Bree, sitting beside him on the loveseat, with Addie curled over her feet. He was beginning to think that his dog, Addie, loved Bree more than him, but that thought didn't make him unhappy. Addie had good taste, and since Bree loved Addie, all was well with him.

Judith watched Booker take in the room before answering. Once again, Judith thought that the Ruby Sister's circle might have grown too big to meet in her living room. But right now, it was familiar, and that's what they all wanted.

Besides, today, with another cold winter wind blowing outside, it was the best place to be. If they all had to stay over again, it would just be the biggest slumber party they ever had. And after all that had happened, no one would mind. Besides, she also knew that the people in this room would need to be the ones who would step up and help Spring Falls recover.

Judith sighed to herself and held Bruce's hand tighter, trying not to get distracted by her worries about what Booker had asked her to do, and Bruce had already encouraged her to do. They both wanted her to run for mayor in the special election that was to be held within the next month.

It was the last thing she had ever wanted for herself, but she loved Spring Falls, and she knew she'd have to eventually say yes. *But please, God,* she said to herself, *not tonight. Don't make me choose tonight. Let me have a few more days alone with my friends.*

Everyone was in Judith's living room thanks to Nancy, who had once again made all the phone calls to get them there. Booker and Judith understood the importance of sharing all that they knew about what had happened with this group all at once. With Spring Falls buzzing with speculation, they wanted to prevent distorted tales from spreading. This group had the influence to quell the rumors and restore the trust that Spring Falls would recover.

Everyone was present, including Mimi and Janet. The only people who had not come were Mary, Seth, and baby Rho. Mary had thought it was best to stay home in case the storm got worse. They knew Bree would fill them in later.

Now, as was their custom, after eating their fill of pizza, the Ruby Sisters and friends had all gathered to learn all that they could about what had happened, and what they could do to put things right again.

But in order to do that, they needed answers to big questions, like who had killed Marshall. After all, wasn't that how all of this had started? Marshall had retired and then was killed before he could escape to the life in paradise he had been planning for years.

It was Bruce, instead of Booker, who finally answered Marsha's question, because he was the one who had figured it out.

"His son was Leon Price."

The room erupted. Bruce waited until the room was quiet, and Marsha asked the next question.

"The guy who has the company that cleans up half the town's businesses and after every event?"

Bruce nodded, and then everyone started asking questions at the same time. "Did Marshall know it had been his son who had pushed him down the stairs? Had he even known that Leon Price was his son?"

*His son,* Judith thought, *who is so much like Marshall. Maybe on a smaller scale, but perhaps, given the chance, he could have become as powerful as his father.*

Booker raised his hand, and when that didn't work to quiet the room, Addie barked once, and everyone laughed, quieted down, and turned to Booker.

"Here's what we know. Yes, Leon pushed Marshall down the stairs. It's not clear that it was on purpose. He says that it wasn't. He was there to collect his last check and found Marshall packed and heading out of town. When he saw how empty the house was, he figured Marshall was not coming back.

"They argued. Marshall fell down the stairs. Leon panicked and left."

"Taking Marshall's computer?" Cindy asked.

"No, that was Margaret. She had gone over to say goodbye, found Marshall at the bottom of the stairs, and realized the same thing that Leon had: Marshall was not planning on coming back. So, knowing what Marshall had on his computer, she took it so no one else would find it.

"And no. It's doubtful that Marshall knew Leon was his son, because even Leon didn't know. When we told him, he said we were liars, but the DNA evidence proves it to be true. Maybe all this wouldn't have happened if either one of them had known. As it is, it's a tragedy for everyone concerned."

"Except for Pedro and his family. They can stay in their homes," Emma said. "Was it Leon who took me to the cabin?"

"It was. He didn't know what else to do when he spotted you walking through the development. Not a well thought out plan."

Judith listened with a growing awareness that in truth, she didn't have a choice. Maybe years before, she could have stopped all this when she worked for Marshall, if she had understood what Marshall was doing.

But she was young and inexperienced then, and maybe a little afraid of Marshall and his power. But now there was no excuse. She had to say yes to Booker; otherwise she wouldn't be able to live with herself.

Letting go of Bruce's hand, she stood. Everyone turned to look. Bruce smiled up at her, giving her strength. He knew what she was going to say.

"Booker asked me to run for mayor."

"Of course he did," Marsha said. "And of course you are."

Everyone laughed, clapped and stood up to hug her. It was the beginning of the town's rebuilding, and they would be right beside her, making sure she had what she needed to make it happen.

# Epilogue

April had requested a quiet party with only the Ruby Sisters for her birthday. They could celebrate with everyone else another time. She loved having the huge crowd that gathered now for events, but this time, she just wanted her closest friends with her. It had been too long since it was just the five of them.

The next day, as a present to herself, she was going to Canada to see her daughter and grandchildren. Her son Robert, who had gone back to traveling the world, would meet her there, so the whole family would be together. That too had been too long, and her heart was so full of happiness at the thought that she felt as if she would explode with joy.

April had already decided that if—and it was a big if—her family brought up her husband Ron, she would ask them to remember only anything good about their time together. She would allow no one to talk about his life as a serial killer. She knew that the pain of that discovery would never leave them, and no one needed to reopen that wound.

If someone had told them it was possible to live with a person with an evil heart and not know it, they wouldn't have believed it. Then. Now her family knew that it was.

Before the party, April and Marsha had stood in the studio in the Ruby House, holding cups of coffee, and looked through the budding maple tree into town. They talked about all the changes that had happened to them in the past few years.

And it all started because Bree's husband had written a letter to all of them before he died, asking them to help his wife. That last gift had changed all their lives more than anyone could have dreamed.

Because of that letter, Marsha had come back to Spring Falls. And met the father she thought had abandoned her. She now knew and accepted how much someone had loved her all along. Her closed heart had opened, and now she spread love to all her students as if they were her own. Despite living a few hours apart, her relationship with Nicky, who had courageously revealed Ron Page's secret, had strengthened over the past year. Maybe someday they would live together, but for now, this was perfect for both of them.

"Ready?" Marsha asked April, thinking how much she would miss her while she was gone. They were holding the party at Bree's house. And although sometimes the second of May was chilly in Pennsylvania, this year it was warm and sunny, so they had moved the party outside to Bree's garden.

April and Marsha pulled up in front of Bree's house at the same time as Cindy. Seeing April, Cindy bounced out of the car and, yelling "Happy Birthday," ran over to hug her friend. Cindy's life had changed too, and it showed.

Judith, watching the greetings from the window in Bree's living room, thought Cindy looked radiant. With Daniel in her life, and her paintings now selling all over the world, Cindy's dreams had come true.

Dreams that only Judith had known about. Dreams Cindy had reluctantly shared with Judith during their Monday morning coffees when they were the only two Ruby Sisters left in town. Bree had moved away, and no one knew where she had gone. April had moved with Ron and never came back. Their only contact was a phone call once in a while.

Marsha had moved to try her hand at being a star on Broadway, and when that didn't work out, she hadn't come back to Spring Falls. Instead, she had opened a dance studio in New York State and only reconnected once in a while.

"It's amazing, isn't it?" Bree said, coming to stand beside Judith at the window.

"And all because of Paul's letter," Judith answered, turning to her friend. "Your husband's last gift to you, and us, changed all our lives. Without the letters he wrote, none of you would have returned. I would not have met Bruce. You and Booker wouldn't have found each other again, and you wouldn't have found the daughter you thought you had lost forever."

Bree leaned against Judith, letting herself drift back to how it felt after Paul died. She had never felt such despair in her life. It was so deep that the only time she opened her door and stepped outside was to get her mail. She had stopped writing, stopped speaking, and stopped bathing. And then Cindy had rescued her and brought her home.

The two of them stood together as they watched their friends come up the walk, and then, brushing tears from their eyes, opened the front door to let them in, saying "Happy Birthday" as hugs were exchanged.

Later, after all the cake and ice cream had been devoured, songs sung, memories shared, and plans made for the future, Cindy joined Judith as she stood watching.

"You're tired, aren't you?"

"Is it that obvious?"

"Probably not to others, but after all, for years, it was just you and me. And now look. You're the mayor trying to put a town back together. But the truth is, Judith, you have been doing that for years for everyone. Your clients, your friends, and now you've just expanded your reach."

Judith turned and sat down on a nearby bench, and Cindy sat with her, and Bree walked over to join them sitting on the other side of Judith.

Smiling at the two of them, she said, "It's so much harder than I thought it would be. So many things were wrong underneath the surface. Marshall and Margaret had their fingers into almost everything. It's like pulling out a weed that looks like it's only on the surface, but its roots spread out everywhere.

"Then there's the politics. And divisions. I don't like it. Not at all. I have to fight every day for people to do the right thing and find a reason for them to choose it. What happened to knowing the right thing for yourself? Why do I have to show it to them? I'm tired even though it's only been a few months, yet it feels like years."

Cindy reached over to hold Judith's hand as Bree smiled and spread open her arms to encompass the garden.

"Remember this place? It looked good on the surface, but when I started working on it, I found the same thing. Weeds everywhere. It was a mess. I wanted to give up.

"But it had good things in it too. Like this tree. You have good things in this town. Like the Ruby Sisters and everyone who works with us. Good people outnumber the bad or confused people. This is something we all need to remember. Joy is stronger than sorrow. We've proved that together, haven't we?"

Judith nodded and looked out at Bree's garden filled with spring flowers and remembered what it looked like before. Pretty. But this was beautiful. Maybe Bree was right. Once the mess was cleaned up, Spring Falls would be even lovelier to live in.

Reaching out to hold Judith's other hand, Bree added, "It won't take forever, Judith. You and Tanner can rebuild the town, and when he's ready, you can step down and he can take over. In the meantime, you always have the Ruby Sisters."

Judith nodded, grateful to her friend, who had been through the worst of times but still spread joy and love wherever she went.

"Ruby Sisters forever, right?"

"Yes," said Judith, thinking how all her friends were like flowers in the garden of life.

Then they reached up and touched their necklaces, which held a single ruby. As they did, a beam of light streamed through the tree, and Bree could have sworn that all five rubies lit up on each of the sisters' necklaces.

And given what they had all been through and learned, Bree didn't think that was impossible. Standing and spreading out her arms to include the garden, her friends, and the town, Bree said, "Thank you, Paul."

For a moment, all five of them paused at those words, and bowed their heads. Then, a soft breeze carrying the smells of spring ruffled their hair, and they laughed and hugged each other. If all their years together had taught them anything, it was that life was hard. But it was worth it.

# Author Note

Thank you for reading this book in the *Ruby Sisters* series. This is the fifth series I've written, and it's especially precious to me because it focuses on a community of women who endure and thrive together.

Sometimes I've named characters after women who have affected my life. Sometimes I have woven tiny stories that happened to me into the books. In this book, the Ruby Sisters wear a dance sweatshirt I designed for one of my beta readers, who shared it with her friends. However, all along, it's been each member of the Ruby Sisters who have told these stories, and I have only listened and written them down.

To me, that's the joy of writing—letting the story unfold and doing my best to tell it truthfully.

I dedicated this last book to my mother, Celeste Cecilia Juneau Lewis. A few weeks before she passed away, I had taken the book before this one, *As If It Was Real*, to her. While cleaning her room, I found it by her bed, waiting to be read next. I wish I could deliver this one to her because she was my biggest vocal fan.

She kept promising me that someday I would be a best-selling author, and she was sure that at least this series would someday be a Hallmark movie. From her lips to God's ears, and now that she is even closer to those ears, I hope that someday her dream about me will come true.

If you enjoyed this book, and any of the books in the *Ruby Sisters* series, would you do me the biggest favor ever and leave an honest review at your favorite book site? And tell your friends? Perhaps tell them that my mother sent you, because maybe, just maybe, she did.

You can find all my books here: BecaLewis.com

# Acknowledgements

I could never write a book without the help of my friends and my book community. Thank you, Jet Tucker, Jamie Lewis, Barbara Budan, and Diana Cormier for taking the time to do the final reader proof. You are a loyal and much-loved reader team. You can't imagine how much I appreciate it.

A huge thank you to Laura Moliter for her fantastic book editing.

Thank you to every other member of my Book Community who helps me make so many decisions that help the book be the best book possible.

Thank you to all the people who tell me they love to read these stories. Those random comments from friends and strangers are more valuable than gold.

And as always, thank you to my beloved husband, Del, for being my daily sounding board, for putting up with all my questions, my constant need to want to make things better, and for being the love of my life, in more than just this one lifetime.

**Connect with me online:**

Facebook: https://www.facebook.com/becalewiscreative
Instagram: https://instagram.com/becalewis
Twitter: http://twitter.com/becalewis
LinkedIn: https://linkedin.com/in/becalewis
Youtube: https://www.youtube.com/c/becalewis

# Also By Beca

**The Rivers of Time Series: Women's Lit, Friendship, Small Town, Mystery, Magical Realism, Small Town Fiction**
*The Returning, The Awakening, The Rising*

***Follow Me Here:*** **Women's Lit, Friendship, Small Town, Mystery, Magical Realism, Small Town Fiction**

**The Ruby Sisters Series: Women's Lit, Friendship, Mystery, Small Town Fiction**
*A Last Gift, After All This Time, And Then She Remembered, As If It Was Real, Almost Innocent*

**Stories From Doveland: Women's Lit, Friendship, Small Town, Mystery, Magical Realism, Small Town Fiction**
*Karass, Pragma, Jatismar, Exousia, Stemma, Paragnosis, In-Between, Missing, Out Of Nowhere*

**The Return To Erda Series: Fantasy**
*Shatterskin, Deadsweep, Abbadon, The Experiment*

**The Chronicles of Thamon: Fantasy**
*Banished, Betrayed, Discovered, Wren's Story*

**The Shift Series: Spiritual Self-Help**
*Living in Grace: The Shift to Spiritual Perception*
*The Daily Shift: Daily Lessons From Love To Money*
*The 4 Essential Questions: Choosing Spiritually Healthy Habits*
*The 28 Day Shift To Wealth: A Daily Prosperity Plan*
*The Intent Course: Say Yes To What Moves You*
*Imagination Mastery: A Workbook For Shifting Your Reality*
*Right Thinking: A Thoughtful System for Healing*
*Perception Mastery: Seven Steps To Lasting Change*
*Blooming Your Life: How To Experience Consistent Happiness*

**Perception Parables: Very short stories**
*Love's Silent Sweet Secret: A Fable About Love*
*Golden Chains And Silver Cords: A Fable About Letting Go*

**Advice / Journals**
*A Woman's ABC's of Life: Lessons in Love, Life, and Career from*
*Those Who Learned The Hard Way*
*The Daily Nudge(s): So When Did You First Notice*

# About Beca

Beca writes books she hopes will change people's perceptions of themselves and the world, and open possibilities to things and ideas that are waiting to be seen and experienced.

At sixteen, Beca founded her own dance studio. Later, she received a Master's Degree in Dance in Choreography from UCLA and founded the Harbinger Dance Theatre, a multimedia dance company, while continuing to run her dance school.

After graduating—to better support her three children—Beca switched to the sales field, where she worked as an employee and independent contractor in many industries, excelling in each while perfecting and teaching her Shift System and writing books.

She joined the financial industry in 1983 and became an Associate Vice President of Investments at a major stock brokerage firm. She was a licensed Certified Financial Planner for over twenty years.

This diversity, along with a variety of life challenges, helped fuel the desire to share what she's learned by writing and speaking, hoping it will make a difference in other people's lives.

Beca grew up in State College, PA, with the dream of becoming a dancer and then a writer. She carried that dream forward as she fulfilled a childhood wish by moving to Southern California in 1968. Beca told her family she would never move back to the cold.

After living there for thirty-one years, she met her husband, Delbert Lee Piper, Sr., at a retreat in Virginia, and everything changed. They decided to find a place they could call their own, which sent them off traveling around the United States. They lived and worked in a few different places before returning to live in the cold once again near Del's family in a small town in Northeast Ohio, not too far from State College.

When not working and teaching together, they love to visit and play with their combined family of eight children and five grandchildren, walk, read, study, do yoga or taiji, feed birds, and work in their garden.

9 7 9 8 9 8 7 9 0 8 8 6 0